UNBOUND

A COLLECTION OF ELEVEN SHORT STORIES

THE D20 AUTHORS

CONTENTS

FOREWORD

In 2020, our group of intrepid authors published their debuts during a global pandemic. Book publishing is a roller coaster at the best of times, and global lockdowns and an ever-rising death toll weren't exactly a great addition to the mix. The silver lining was that our group of newbie authors banded together (in part, through sheer desperation) over Facebook, Zoom and – when we finally could – in person. We became known as the 'D20 Authors' (aka Debut 2020 Authors), and have remained a supportive and active group ever since.

In 2022, we released our first short story anthology, *UnLocked*. We were overwhelmed by the response to this collection, with glowing reviews, fantastic sales, and a CWA Dagger shortlisting for one of the stories: *The Tears of Venus* by Victoria and

Delilah Dowd. Just as importantly, we have been able to donate all of our profits from *UnLocked* to our nominated charity, The Trussell Trust (www. trusselltrust.org), and as our sales of this first anthology continue, we will continue to support this important cause. If you were one of the many people who bought, read and reviewed our first D20 collection – thank you. (And if you haven't yet got your hands on a copy, you can find it in e-book and paperback here: https://www.amazon.-co.uk/UnLocked-captivating-collection-stories-Authors-ebook/dp/B0BK1K74WY.)

Since our debuts were released in 2020, our group has gone on to publish many more books, win many awards, and support and champion one another through the various ups and downs of our publishing journeys. Being a professional author is always a rocky road, with as much disaster as there is triumph. Yet authors are some of the kindest and most supportive people I know, and I believe our D20 group of authors is no exception. And because we just can't seem to get enough of writing, publishing and satisfying our readers, last year we decided to create and release a second short story anthology, *UnBound* – which is what you hold in your hands now.

A project like this is always a labour of love

and, once again, it has been a great team effort. Huge thanks to the amazing authors who have contributed stories to this collection, as well as to all of the additional members of our D20 group – and beyond – who have helped with editing, research, cover design, title brainstorming, promotion and general enthusiastic cheerleading of the project.

You will find details about each contributing writer at the end of their individual stories – do check out their books via the links provided (or at the very least go and say hello to them on social media; they will be delighted to hear from you). I hope that from dipping into the pieces in this anthology you will be inspired to track down the full range of brilliant books our D20 authors have published over the years. To help, we have collected all of our published books in one handy place, which you can access via our affiliate link: https://uk.bookshop.org/shop/TheD20Authors.

For this anthology, we are delighted to be supporting the adult literacy charity Read Easy (CC 1151288). Read Easy provides free, one-to-one reading coaching programmes for adults, supported by two thousand-plus volunteers, with the vision that every adult who wants to read, can. We are honoured to be supporting them and you can find out more about their work here: https://readeasy. org.uk/.

Finally, thank you so much for picking up and reading this collection. I really do hope you enjoy it.

Philippa East
August 2024

THE REUNION

CAT WALKER

'I never thought you'd be the type to come to the school reunion, mate!' he shouts over in a fake southern accent – the kind people use when they're trying to impress and kid on that they've moved up in the world. But I can hear underneath that he's still got a twang of round here. I look up, shocked that he'd be talking to me, let alone calling me 'mate'. But it's not me he's talking to, of course. It's Sean, who's appeared from nowhere, barging past me like we're still in the dinner queue. Like I'm not even there.

'Couldn't miss the big announcement, could I?' Sean laughs. 'Big night tonight, buddy!'

Robbo punches Sean on the arm with a smile. Not the way he used to punch me, I might add. Standing there in his rented tux like he's Kanye or something. Oh, this evening is going to be sweet, I think.

I walk past them both and neither even gives me a second glance. Five years in the same classrooms and I don't see the slightest hint of recognition in their eyes. But they will remember me. Everyone will remember me after tonight.

I look around the old school hall – the scuffed lines taped to the wooden floor, the climbing bars folded back against the wall, the basketball hoops with just a hint of string left, like something your nan knitted after one too many sherries at Christmas. Nothing's changed. It even smells the same – that curious mixture of sweat, must and over-boiled cabbage.

There aren't many people here yet, so I take a plastic cup of dubious-looking punch from the big washing up bowl on the folding table at one end of the hall and feign interest in the pictures lining the walls. It's the usual mixture of crap artwork and team photos. You know the type; the first XI football, hockey and cricket teams that kind of blend into one as it's usually the same kids who are good at all sports.

I know I won't be in any of them. I wasn't one of those kids. I didn't really like team sports. I wasn't really any good at them. I preferred gaming and, you know, just keeping my head down and getting decent grades, otherwise I would've caught it from Mum. She was always telling me how much it cost her to send me to a 'good school' and she didn't want me wasting my time playing stupid ball games. So I kept my head down and kept out of trouble. Got the grades. Good enough to get myself to uni, briefly, and that's not a given round here.

My eyes travel over the photos, and then I spot her. The reason I'm here. Front and centre of the netball team. Blonde ponytail perfectly aligned over her right shoulder, her manicured fingernails holding a ball outstretched as if she's about to launch it through the net without touching the sides. Short skirt ironed and hitched up at the waistband to reveal a few more inches of her long, golden legs. Even in faded polychrome she looks perfect. I can hardly wait to see her tonight. She'll knock spots off all of the other girls in the room, even after all this time. And I'll be the luckiest guy in the world.

In many ways all of my life has been leading up to this moment, tonight. My mind wanders back to the day I first laid eyes on her. We had been in the same boat, metaphorically speaking; both joining the school in third year after most of the friendship groups had already formed strong bonds. Both of us new to the area. We naturally drifted together. Everything was perfect right from the beginning. We saw each other every day, took the same classes, chose the same food from the canteen, and were rarely out of sight of one another.

Here she is in another photo; Bugsy Malone, the school musical. She was Tallulah, of course. She had the most amazing flapper dress you ever saw. She wore this feather boa that kept tickling my nose. Ha! I still remember that song she sang. Weird how some things just stay with you. 'My name is

Tallulah, and soon I'll be gone', 'I'll never say goodbye', 'but you won't forget me'. OK, so I don't remember all of the words! I wasn't in the show but I worked backstage and watched it every night from the wings before packing away the set, the stray costumes and the feather boa that she left on stage at the end of the night for me to fetch for her.

We were totally inseparable. (Unhealthy, my mum called it, but who cares?) We were young and in love. And I vowed I'd carry that torch forever. I knew from the moment I'd laid eyes on her that she was the one for me. And tonight, finally, it'll all come together. We'll come together, forever. It will definitely be a big night.

I pull myself away from the school musical and the netball team to be confronted by the much less pretty rugby first XV, with Robbo front and centre this time. The cocky captain. Beefy arms folded over a muscular chest. His taut thigh muscles making his shorts look uncomfortably stretched. A big stupid grin on his face. Looking back now, with the benefit of a score of high school movies under my belt, I guess I see that Robbo, Sean and the gang were just acting out the parts of your typical jock: big, muscular and stupid. The opposite of me.

I remember this one time when Robbo tried it on with her, my Tallulah, at the school disco in fourth year. The rugby team had just won some tournament or other so he was celebrating by being a complete dick and kissing all the girls. High on whatever low grade, class C, prescription pills his mates had robbed off their mums and aunties. He'd tried to grab her, right in front of me. Practically stuck his tongue down her throat. So, of course, I thumped him one, right there in front of all his mates. In front of her. What choice did I have?

It was a bad move. His mates dragged me outside and Robbo kicked seven sorts of shit out of me. Calling me a 'Mummy's boy'. Nearly broke my jaw. I was off school for a week. She wasn't even allowed to come and see me 'cause my mum thought it was all her fault. Usual teenage dramas, right? But if Mum thought that would break us apart, she was wrong. It only brought us even closer together. After that, although I was more careful to avoid Robbo, I never let her out of my sight.

I never liked the school holidays, you know. Strange, right? But it was the only time that I didn't get to see her. I'd hang around town, frequenting the kind of shops that I knew she and her friends went to, but it was hit and miss.

I finger the metal inside my pocket and it makes my heart beat a little faster. It grows warmer against my fingers, and I imagine it becoming one with her body heat soon. Blood from her heart line flowing against it. I picture the scene in my head one more time: me walking through the crowd towards her, the sea of bodies parting to let me through. Everyone's eyes on me. On her. On us. I go down on one knee and say the words I've prepared. Ask her the question. Her eyes widen as she looks at me. Her lips part to form an answer.

'Mr Eavis!' Somebody shouts across the hall from just behind me, snapping me out of my reverie and sending an involuntary shiver down my spine.

'Mr Eavis, as I live and breathe!' the guy follows up, striding across the hall to greet the eponymous hero with a huge bear hug. Others follow until Mr Eavis, Ben, is swallowed in a sea of appreciative bodies. Once upon a time, I would have been the first among them, but tonight I have a greater goal. Though I'm glad that he's here. Really glad, in fact.

I was going to tell you a bit more about how the romance with my beloved developed, but now that 'Call me Ben' Mr Eavis is here, I think I should probably tell you a bit about that one now. I don't mean it like that. Don't get me wrong. There was no 'romance' between Ben and myself. But he did give me my other love. A love of guns.

Oh yes, I used to love the smell of cordite in the morning! But if I'd told you that upfront, you'd have me down as some sort of nutter. A gun freak. That's not what this is. That's not who I am. Although I've got to admit, if you were going to commit a school shooting, this would actually be the perfect setting.

But, I digress. Let me tell you about Ben. Mr Eavis. The much-loved geography teacher who doubled as the major of the school's Army Cadet Force. Oh yes, I told you it was a posh school. Or, if not posh, then fee-paying at least, as my mum would never let me forget.

Good old Ben. Everybody loved Ben. Great marksman too. If you can believe it, we had a target shooting range dug underneath our ACF hut. Ben spotted early on that I was a good shot. I think I was just a controlled kind of person, good at commanding my breath – very important for a good marksman. He trained me up to be the best in our shooting team. We won competitions all over the country. I mean, it wasn't that much of a contest really, as few schools had their own ranges. But Ben was super proud of us anyway, and that meant a lot. He was the coolest teacher in school by miles. Spent a lot of time with us older boys just hanging out at the ACF hut after school, talking about guns and offering his advice. 'Call me Ben' was his nickname, 'cause of how he liked to pal up to us. We spent a lot of time together when I wasn't with her.

I wasn't the only one. Robbo was mad keen on guns too, but not in a disciplined way like me. He was hot-headed; couldn't keep control. It made him second best as a marksman. He could never stand that I came out better than him. I guess that's why I was Ben's favourite, and why Robbo picked on me relentlessly.

If you ask me, Robbo had an unhealthy obsession with guns. Rifles and uniforms were more to him than messing about; they were a calling. It was no wonder that he joined up straight after school. I heard he got into the Royal Artillery as a gunner. Did a few tours in Afghanistan. That'd be enough to send anyone off their nut. If you were thinking about who out of all of us would be most likely to commit a mass shooting, it'd be Robbo for sure.

Even as I'm thinking about him, Robbo strides into my field of vision, walking straight up to Mr Eavis and giving him an awkward man hug, slapping his back as if he's got something clinging there that needs killing. Ben returns the hug and mouths something that looks like 'congratulations' but, as he turns, his eyes lock on mine across the room, and my breath catches in my throat.

An unwanted memory shoots into my consciousness. Ben lying beside me in the claustrophobic rifle range, his hands on mine as he shows me how to grip the rifle just so. I can feel his breath on my cheek; it smells of cigarettes and chewing gum mingling with his Lynx aftershave. It makes me want to gag but I hold steady, keeping my eyes on the target twenty-five yards away down that narrow tunnel. He inches closer until he's practically on top of me. I know what's coming but keep staring at that target like my life depends on it. If I can still make the shot, get the bullseye, then perhaps he'll leave me alone, I think. You don't need to coach someone who's already perfect, right? But he doesn't stop. And maybe you'd think the fact that I have a gun in my hands would deter him, but it's exactly the opposite as it turns out. You can't turn a rifle round in a shooting range tunnel. You can't really move at all.

A sudden shout nearby makes me jump. The room has been filling up while I've been reminiscing about the 'good old days'. Mostly people are gathering in little gaggles. Even after all these years, the same old cliques seem to be attracting their members like flies to shit: the cool ones, the sporty ones, the pretty ones, the rich ones, the trendy geeks, the untrendy geeks. I walk over to the DJ to see what horrendous music is going to form the backdrop to tonight's show.

I would have left Gun Club but Mum insisted I stay. She thought the military discipline was good for me, and she wasn't someone that you could easily argue with. A single mum who brought up her only son with a zeal you'd rarely find outside of the Old Testament. Besides, she was also under the spell of parents' favourite, Mr Eavis.

I walk past a group of giggling girls in grown-up dresses.

'Isn't that the creep that used to follow S ... around?' One of them whispers a little too drunkenly not to be overheard. But I don't see who she's talking about, and gossip doesn't interest me. Only she interests me.

She has been the focal point of my life now for more than ten years. Everything has been about her. She was the one good thing about school, about life. The only thing that kept me sane when everything was happening with Ben. But I never told her. Could never find the right time, or the right words. I wonder now, I don't know, maybe if I had told her ... Maybe, I think that maybe, she would have understood. She would have ... seen me.

But she never saw me at all.

I didn't exist for her.

If she had seen me, I mean *really* seen me, she would maybe have not gone off with Robbo the rugby player. Robbo the jock. She would maybe have spent all that time with me and not him, and I wouldn't have spent all that time in Gun Club. She would have been with me and not waiting for him to come back from shooting people in Afghanistan. She would have seen that it's Robbo who's the creep, the psycho, not me. She would be announcing her engagement to ME and not Robbo.

The Boomtown Rats start to play through the sound system. That one about not liking Mondays. It's nearly time.

Robbo's looking a bit nervous which is so very unlike him. Is he wondering whether she's stood him up? Whether she's changed her mind? He scans the room and suddenly spots me propping up the makeshift bar. His expression changes into something like disdain. I can almost hear the thought going through his head: Mummy's boy! Well not any more, Robbo. Oh yes, Mummy had tears in her eyes when I left for the party, but they most certainly weren't pride.

So, what is going to happen tonight? How is it

all going to end? Well, I told you, didn't I? That this was the perfect setting …

But, well, as I also told you, I'm not that kind of guy. Am I?

But if I was. *IF* I was to … Well, these things have to be planned, don't they. You can't just spontaneously decide to up and, you know …

So if I *was* to have decided to do something like that, well then I suppose I would have kept my copy of the key to the gun cupboard. The one that Ben gave me for my 'extra practices'. Then I would have had to sneak into school, maybe sometime last month, in the school holidays, to check that they hadn't changed the lock. And if they hadn't, well, shame on you, Mr Eavis. The Health and Safety Committee would be appalled.

Then I guess I would have made a return trip the night before the big event. Last night. And I would have taken a couple of the new L98A2 Cadet GP Rifles the school had purchased since I was there. Of course I would have also had to google how these worked, as they're very different beasts from the old converted Lee Enfield I was taught on. But they would have been better for the job in hand, as they're self-loading, rapid-fire weapons with a 30-round magazine and 5.56mm bullets capable of doing a lot more damage than a single-shot bolt-action .22 like the Lee Enfield.

I think it's pretty likely that, if I *were* planning this, I would have also grabbed Ben's prize Walther PPK German pistol. The one that was totally illegal for him to store in there but which he loved to show off to his chosen ones because he thought it made him look like James Bond. He was always adamant that it had been deactivated but I guess that, if you knew the right people, it would probably be pretty easy to reactivate if it hadn't been done too well. Plus, it can take the same .22 rounds that the Lee Enfield takes, so ammo wouldn't be an issue.

And I think that I would probably take one of the good old Lee Enfields as well, just for old time's sake. Because it was my first love. And a first love for a first love would probably seem quite poetic.

So I guess then I would have brought the fully-loaded guns from the armoury up to the school hall and hidden them somewhere they'd be available for easy access. Perhaps in that cupboard over there, where the balls and bibs are stored. But not all together. More strategically placed. Like, one in the cupboard at the other end of the hall where the footie goals live, and one with the badminton nets at the other side. And the spare ammo in the cubby hole where the keys are kept, here, just behind me.

Of course I would have already removed some of the keys, the ones I needed to lock the doors, and meticulously planned my 'route' for maximum efficiency, ending up with Ben's loaded pistol and my trusty single bolt-action converted Lee Enfield, and the last bullet here in my pocket.

I would have also sent Ben a note telling him that I wanted to talk to him to make sure that he came. And I'd have planned it so that I picked up the same rifle that Robbo had been using that day for his rifle practice at the range. (I told you he was a gun nut.) I know that Ben still lets him in to do that in the holidays. And I'd use gloves, of course.

Then all I would have had to do was show up on the night and wait for everyone to arrive. *IF* that's what I had in mind. *IF* that's what I was planning, that is.

Ah, here she comes now …

CAT WALKER'S DEBUT NOVEL, *The Scoop*, described by LoveReading.co.uk as 'amusing, poignant, insightful and even educational – a real road trip to savour' was published in March 2020 by RedDoor Press and longlisted for The Guardian's Not The Booker Prize that year. Cat also writes poetry and her first collection, *Holding My Breath to keep the love inside*, was published by Trafford Publishing in 2008. She is currently working on a collection of short stories. Cat lives on the Sussex coast with her wife and son. You can find out more about her via the links below:

www.catwalkerauthor.com

Twitter/X: @CatWalkerAuthor

Instagram: @thescoopbycatwalker

Facebook: @thescoopbycatwalker

TINY HANDS

ANDREINA CORDANI

There is a streak of something on the shoulder of Mirabel's hoodie. It's pinkish white, crusted, and when she comes in to hug me it smells faintly sour.

'Oh that.' She scrapes at it irritably with a fingernail. Casually, as if she doesn't realise how much these little details hurt. 'Bloody fromage frais. Riley smears it everywhere.'

I turn away, bracing myself for the wave of sadness I know is coming. It's all been too much. First, the ride over here in a car full of grubby toys and crushed Pom-Bear crisps. Then her incessant chatter – Riley this, Riley that. *He's talking now, saying full sentences. He's hard work, having tantrums. You can't reason with them at this age, you know?* She doesn't seem to know how each detail stings like a scalpel-cut.

Beatrice would have been two last week. There would have been a party at Cuddles Soft Play, with her and Riley throwing themselves down the Big Slide and smearing fromage frais over each other. At the end of the day I'd be worn down and brittle, the house a tip, bickering with Marc over who was the most tired. Grumbling when she creeps into our bed at night, breaking our sleep. People say the toddler years are tough, but I'd looked forward to them the most. The total immersion in motherhood; their big personality that takes over your life.

I'll never have that now. Instead, I have this. I balance the box I'm carrying on my knee and unlock my new, grey front door, letting it swing open into a wide hallway.

'Wow, it's incredible,' Mirabel says. 'I'd kill to live in a place like this.'

Well, someone did have to die to land me here.

It's the modern house I dreamt of when I was young and single: stripped wood floors, white walls, large floor-to-ceiling windows. Beyond them I can see the slow-moving river swollen from the rain and choked with long, green weeds. I always wanted to live near water, but I couldn't have done that with a young child. This is not a family home, it is a private retreat. It's for someone who has accepted the fact that she is going to live alone.

Mirabel senses it. She reaches out and lays a hand on my shoulder, and when she speaks her voice is full of encouragement.

'Good for you.'

I fight not to flinch.

So brave. That's what everyone says to me. To lose a baby and then for Marc to walk out so soon after. *So strong.*

People say that only true friends stick around when things like this happen, but you also get your fair share of rubberneckers. People who parachute in with a frozen lasagne and a bunch of opinions. Who cast Marc as the bad guy to my face, then secretly tell their partners that I went completely doolally after Bea's death and it's a wonder Marc stayed as long as he did. Who tried to get me to open up, telling me it would make me feel better when really they're just hoping for titbits to pass on to the rest of the NCT WhatsApp group.

For all her tone-deaf Riley chat, at least Mirabel isn't one of those. She helps me unload the last of my things, and there are pathetically few of them. It's amazing how little ordinary stuff matters when you've lost everything.

'There must be a kettle in here somewhere,' she says, rummaging through a box, pulling out one item after another until …

'Oh!' I hear the awkwardness in her voice, and I know what she's found. She's holding a nest of bubble wrap in her hands and looks deeply uncomfortable.

'Give them to me,' I snap. I look down and check they're both there; nothing chipped or broken, each miniature finger perfectly intact.

'They're …'

'Ceramic casts of Beatrice's hands, yes.'

Mirabel presses her lips together and I turn away, unwilling to see her lack of understanding. Few people seem to get it. Even Marc, who I had believed to be my partner in pain, had called them ghoulish when I had them done, it was one of the first things we fought about. But I had just wanted to keep a little part of her, this girl who should have been mine for life.

This was the only way I could ever hold her hand.

Now I'm alone, at least I can keep them by my bed; reach for them in the night without anyone judging me.

After finishing her tea, Mirabel is gone, driving her sticky, messy car off to collect Riley from nursery. I find a wine glass, pour myself some room-temperature white and sit in the fading light, stroking Beatrice's tiny white palm.

THE FIRST FEW weeks in the house pass quietly. We are in the deathly-grey shades of January and I allow the days to blur into one. Working from home at my desk by the window, shuffling about in grubby slippers, the silence wrapped around me like a chill, comfortless blanket.

At times the cold seeps into me and I end up working in bed under the quilt, grateful for my laptop's warmth. At night I huddle under layers of bedding, Beatrice's hand in mine, warmed up by the heat of my body.

The tidiness of living alone is strange. Beatrice never got a chance to make a mess, but Marc was loud and slovenly, leaving a trail of used mugs and damp towels behind him. It's been a long time since I've put something away and it's simply stayed there.

Which is why I notice the crumbs.

Just a few bits of digestive in the middle of the kitchen island, even though I have not eaten a biscuit since I wiped it down earlier. I wipe it again, tell myself I'm mad, but the next morning I see some water pooled on the floor outside the shower. Small, perfectly formed. It looks like a footprint.

I shiver, but then pull myself back to the real world, sliding the bath-mat over the puddle with my foot, telling myself there's a rational explanation. But I can't think of one, because I just know there is someone else in this house with me.

Someone with tiny feet.

I should be afraid, but I'm not. Instead, my heart is fluttering with something like hope. I leave a biscuit out on the kitchen island, with a glass of milk beside it, feeling faintly foolish. I try not to sit watching it all day.

That night I wake to the light pad-pad of footsteps. I lie still in the darkness and feel the quilt lift gently. Something small and chilly slides in next to me. I can hear breathing, the slow, even breath of a drowsy child falling asleep. I can't move, too afraid to turn around and see whatever is there.

Instead, I whisper, 'You don't need to be afraid, I won't hurt you.'

AT FIRST I wonder if this … *presence?* … is Beatrice, who has somehow grown from babyhood and found her way back to me. But then, as I come through to the lounge one morning, I see a child running off around the corner, a flick of brown hair, rat-tailed with wet, and a dress with yellow sunflowers on it. I would know my daughter anywhere, even in the afterlife, and that is not her.

But it's another child, lost and alone.

It takes me a while to get her to trust me. I buy Kinder chocolate and Pom-Bears. I leave CBeebies on in the lounge. I always said I'd never let Bea watch television until she was at least four but the mesmerising effect it has on this girl is helpful. It allows me to get close.

She doesn't notice until I'm cross-legged on the floor next to her. I hold out a small Peppa Pig toy I bought from the corner shop and she takes it, her insubstantial fingers closing around the pink plastic. I marvel at the perfection of her short little fingernails and feel sad at the mud engrained underneath them. I'm fairly sure this girl drowned in the river outside and has washed back to me somehow. Perhaps if I had bothered chatting to my neighbours, I'd have found out about a shocking local tragedy. If I searched online, I would probably find a newspaper story with a smiling photo and a coroner's report. But I realise I don't want to hear about her life before, to taste the grief of her devastated family. She is mine.

She smiles at me, showing a row of white, perfectly even teeth.

'I'm sorry about what happened to you,' I say. 'You're welcome here.'

So this is what it's like. This is parenthood. Footsteps trail me around the house, cold fingers poke and tickle me when I try to work. Laughter and tears keep me up at night. It is wonderful.

'You look awful,' Mirabel says the next time I

see her, and I beam. I look as wrung-out as she does. I can finally listen to the trials of life with Riley without bitterness swamping me.

When I come home, the girl is waiting just inside, watching the door like a faithful spaniel, and I feel a stab of guilt.

'Sorry. Mummy had to go out.'

There. I've said it – the M-word.

She slips a hand into mine and I feel a longing to hug her. But although she can touch me – jab me with her fingertips or nestle her toes in under my fleecy dressing gown, I can't touch her. It's the one part of parenthood I don't have.

Later, I find myself holding the casts of Bea's hands, stroking the inside of the palm, planting gentle kisses on her fingertips. The girl looks at me quizzically and I explain. *Once upon a time I had another little girl. Smaller than you, and now she is gone.*

Living toddlers have trouble understanding the concept of death, but my girl looks at me solemnly and nods.

She is clever. After a few weeks watching Mr Tumble, she says hello using Makaton sign language and the joy I feel is overwhelming.

I hold out my arms, intending to throw them around her but, of course, I can't. She smiles and catches my wrist in her fingers. The cold is instant, it freezes my skin like Arctic weather. I can feel the warmth being sucked out of me as if she's dug a straw into my flesh and is drinking hungrily. My head swims, my heart pounds and my knees begin to buckle. I panic, pull my hand away with a yelp.

'Please,' I say, 'no.'

She stares at me, hurt flashing in her pale grey eyes.

It's the first time I have ever told her no.

WEEKS PASS. I sing, I invent games, we play hide and seek. There aren't many places to hide in this stark, modern home but she always hides in the same place anyway, under the table. One afternoon, I put blankets over it and make a den underneath. I can hear my laptop beeping on the other side of the room, but it's fine to take a few hours off.

MIRABEL ON MY DOORSTEP, paper cups in hand.

'I've brought coffee!' she gives me a cheery smile that's tight around the edges, squeezes past me through the door – catching sight of the doll's tea party I haven't had time to put away.

'I've been looking after a neighbour's girl,' I say. 'It's why I haven't been in touch, I've been so busy.'

ANDREINA CORDANI

Her smile widens and loosens – relieved there is an explanation for my withdrawal and it's a happy one. We sip coffee and talk about nap times and sticky fingers and whether using sign language makes it easier or harder for kids to learn to speak and I feel like I finally belong, I have something to say. The girl watches us from the corner, hair dripping a puddle on my best cushion – the water always seeps through when she is unsure. Perhaps I shouldn't let Mirabel in next time.

'Just you and me from now on,' I say to my girl later, and she snuggles into bed with me. I can feel her skin, chilly against mine, but it's not as cold as that time she touched my wrist. She reaches forward with one pale, white finger and taps the top of my hand. I open it, show her that I'm holding Bea's cast.

Her face clouds, twisting into anger, and her hand slaps at mine, knocking the cast out of it. My stomach lurches with panic as it bounces onto the mattress. I manage to catch it before it reaches the floor, feeling a flood of relief. Holding the hand to my chest, I meet her gaze, my eyes serious.

'Please don't, these things are precious to me.'

Me, the girl signs.

'You're precious to me too.'

Her smile is beautiful, it makes me ache with happiness, and we drift off to sleep together.

MY ALARM DOESN'T GO off the next morning. I sit up, cursing and heavy with sleep. My feet crunch on biscuit crumbs as I stumble out of bed. It's not until I reach the bathroom that I feel the wet on my sole. My foot is bleeding. They weren't biscuit crumbs.

A hollow opens up in my chest as I go back to my room and see the fragments of ceramic on the floor, smashed into powder. Sobs overwhelm me, pain pulses in my head. I'm curled on the floor screaming with agony and loss. The girl appears next to me, touching me lightly, coldly on the shoulder and I push the feeling away.

'How could you?' I shriek. 'What a monstrous, horrible thing to do. You're …' I'm blind with rage but still parenting, still searching for a word she can understand. 'You're *naughty*.'

Her face crumbles with horror but she needs to learn, she needs boundaries. She needs to know how much this hurts. Bea is lost to me now; I'll never be able to touch her again.

The girl flickers and is gone and, now I'm alone, the rage leaches out of me. I remember Mirabel talking about this, how no matter how good a parent you try to be, you can completely lose it with your child.

'*It happens to us all and we feel awful, but we're only human, right?*'

I'm aching with shame. The loss of the casts cuts me deeply but they're just things. Bea is gone, this girl is here.

I find her under the table as usual. I get in there with her and hand her a biscuit, the only apology I think she can understand.

'You're the most important, precious thing in the world to me,' I say. 'You're my family now.'

She signs: *Hug.*

I open my arms, and she sinks into them – I am dizzy with relief as her hand closes around the top of my arm. Just like before, the cold is painful, but this time I bear it. I deserve this. The cold spreads through my arm and across my shoulders, like daggers cutting right to the bone. I'm shivering madly but still I don't pull away as it spreads through my chest, down my limbs, like being plunged into the river outside. I can't move now, but she is supporting me, gentle and strong as she lowers me onto my back. I feel different now. I'm still cold, but it feels bearable – and then it just feels normal. I look up into the girl's eyes. They're deep brown, her yellow dress is a brighter shade than I have ever seen before. I can see individual freckles on her button-nose. Her greyness is gone and I know her name. It's Imogen.

She smiles, scrambling to her feet in that busy way that toddlers have when they've things to do and people to see. When I stand up, I feel like I've left something behind, but I can't quite place what it is. I glance back and see a bundle of fleecy clothes under the table, two pale bare feet sticking out from pyjama legs. One heel is still slightly bloody from where it trod on something sharp this morning. I don't feel like it's anything to do with me any more.

Imogen hugs me again and I lift her up high, whirl her around like I always wanted to do. Sunlight creeps in through the window and I spin faster and faster, both of us laughing.

I really could do this forever.

BEFORE BECOMING AN AUTHOR, **Andreina Cordani** was a journalist, editor and book reviewer and worked for magazines including *Good Housekeeping*, *Cosmopolitan*, *that's life!* and *Easy Living*. She now lives on the South coast with her lovely family and spends most of her time avoiding them so she can try to write. She is the author of two dark thrillers for young adults, plus the festive whodunnit, *The Twelve Days of Murder*. Her second Christmas book, *Murder at the Christmas Emporium* is out now. You can connect with Andreina via the links below:

www.andreinacordani.com

Twitter/X: @AndreinaCordani

Instagram: @andreinacordani

CATACOMB

VICTORIA DOWD

I turn my story over once again, a pebble polished smooth now. In some ways it's a common tale; every graveyard, crypt and catacomb have their share of ghosts, or some tortured spirit locked in purgatory, a wronged soul seeking revenge, a dark heart bent on redemption. But it's also a rare tale that has left its mark on me.

There is nothing extraordinary about the haunting of our catacombs except that Millicent Greyling's wandering, doomed spirit is that of my murdered great aunt. Her story has haunted me since the day I was born, the curse of her unsolved death hanging about my name like a dark talisman, following me through my school days, trailing out after me into my job in the university library. That little river of intrigue has run beneath every friendship, love affair or mild acquaintance I have ever had. All probing for details of '*The Greyling Mystery*.' Try working in the local history and folklore section with a name like mine.

'Greyling? Like the Greyling Lady? The murdered bride?'

'Yes. Yes. Yes. Great Aunt Millicent was the woman found dead in Exeter's catacombs on her wedding day.'

What makes it more attractive to the ever-

37

expanding true-crime community is, of course, the impossibility of the crime. *The Locked Tomb Mystery* of Exeter's catacombs has fascinated amateur sleuths and the gore-monger press for decades. Sightings of the Greyling Bride are still frequent as she drifts inside her barred tomb, unable to escape, shrouded in folds of grey satin and cobwebs of ripped lace. Some have even reported being able to smell her coppery blood on the air. Others, that her pitiful whimpering can be heard leaking out from that premature tomb.

Millicent Greyling was only eighteen when she was discovered inside the old catacombs. The burial chambers had never proved popular with the people of Exeter. Their grand Egyptian facades hide space for thousands of dead but only fourteen people were ever interred, lonely ghosts left to wander corridors designed for far more spirits. Millicent Greyling had been the unexpected guest.

The dead souls were the only ones to witness her violent, bloody killing. No one could explain how her slaughtered body came to be found inside the catacombs. All the entrances were still locked and barred to the outside world. When they finally gained entrance and reached her corpse, some fifteen feet away from the gate, they unfurled her slim fingers and found she was gripping the key.

There had only ever been two keys to the catacombs in existence. One was lodged with the council, locked in their vaults where it still remained; the other was with the Keeper of the Catacombs who had been holidaying in Scotland with his sister at the time and, being the most dedicated of grave men, he kept it with him at all times.

Millicent's pitiful body was discovered when two lovers had an early morning assignation that did not remain secret for long after their grisly discovery, their names immediately splashed all over every newspaper and forever linked to this terrible tale. The catacombs had not proved popular with the dead, but they did with 'courting couples' as my great grandmother had always called them. This particular young couple's screams could be heard echoing throughout the whole town, she'd said.

She had told it better than anyone. When the alarm went up, the townspeople rushed to the scene to find the gate locked as always. The bloody corpse lay still beyond. The key was duly fetched from the town hall vault. The police, struggling to hold back the gathered crowd, unlocked the gate and pushed open the rusted bars.

Inside, was a desolate, cold scene. Millicent Greyling's abandoned body lay motionless in a tangle of bloodied satin and lace. The groom was sent for much earlier than he should have seen his bride on their wedding day. Great Grandmother said he spent the rest of his days in pilgrimage to those bleak caves, a desperate heart seeking one last view of his phantom bride. A widower before he was ever married. His prophetic, sad tale of loss only added to the legend of her haunting the barren caverns.

There'd been a resurgence in speculation and interest lately. When my beloved great grandmother, Elspeth, slipped away, her sister Millicent's unsolved death was the headline again. There might have been some serendipity if my great grandmother had chosen to be laid to rest out there with the ghost of her sister. But, as Great Granny always said, 'Who the hell wants to spend eternity with the ghost of a murder victim? I deserve some peace in death.'

So we buried Great Granny in a conventional grave, if shovelling earth over our loved ones whilst they lie in a wooden box can ever be called conventional. I will always remember that afternoon, the light vanishing as if she'd rubbed it out herself before she left.

It had been a despondent sky hanging low over the city, with clouds as heavy as our mourning eyes.

Later, my mother found me on the stairs and sat down next to me, placing an old shoebox on her lap.

'She loved you best,' was all she said, her eyes fixed on the peeling wall ahead.

'I …' The words fell away. Denial seemed like an insult.

'Granny left you something.'

My eyes travelled to the box. Its simplicity, the worn cardboard edges and thick layer of dust intriguing.

'Take it.' My mother pushed it onto my lap. The grey dust had marked her black skirt. She paused before brushing it away with a brusque hand. To this day, I don't know if she'd looked inside the box. Either way, she made it clear that this legacy was mine alone now, for good or bad.

I took it to my room, carefully placing it on the dressing table with an attempt at ceremony, and watched it for a while as if there might be some life within. When I lifted the lid, I imagined the scent of Great Grandma lifting from inside, some remnant of her yet to leave.

But what I found in that box seemed to bear no relation to the woman I'd known.

In the ends of that maudlin day, as dusk painted shadows around the faded chintz wallpaper, Great

Granny's favourite apple tree tapped at the window, its branches, bare and gnarled. All the fruit had been left to rot this year.

My eyes fell back to the box, with its old smell of dust and dried out newspapers. On the very top was a note. 'Always count the blessings. EG.' My fingers traced round the ink. Elspeth Greyling. Great Grandmother.

Some small newspaper clippings littered the first layer of the box calling out headlines from another time.

Murdered Bride!

Locked Tomb Mystery

Girl brutally stabbed in the back

No way in! No way out! No weapon found at the scene!

I lifted the slips of paper like relics, placing them carefully on the dressing table, spacing them as if they were fragile bones to reconstruct. There were faded photographs of the catacombs looking no different than they did today, eerie and abandoned, all twined up with the ivy.

But beneath that first layer of newspaper cuttings was something more substantial.

A book.

A diary.

I paused. The dark leather cover and thick

binding gave it an almost sacred look, something not to disturb lightly.

How long had this waited here in silence?

I felt the soft patter of my pulse. As I opened the cover, the black letters were there on that first page, curling into a familiar name.

Millicent Greyling.

She had begun in a definite, bold feminine hand, so innocent of all the gruesome titles she would one day attract.

1ˢᵗ January 1914

My darling has proposed. A gift for the New Year like no other! It will be a summer wedding. He says we must act before war comes. Why must he be so pessimistic? There will be no war.

I paused in the stillness.

The old apple tree rapped at the window again. I drew a sharp breath and held my hand to my chest as if to stop something falling out. There was no more than a feathering of light across the dressing table now. I clicked on the small, fringed lamp and the faces in those newspaper cuttings drifted up from another time, gathering around the light for the reading. Millicent was there, as young as the day she wrote these words. All so innocent. Her secrets lost for so long, now in my hands – for better or worse.

Millicent, whose story had been a spectre in my life, was young again in these pages. She'd not written anything for a few days after that opening entry. I imagined her preoccupied with the excitement and buzz of it all. The joy at the announcement. A time of celebration.

4TH JANUARY

John was a little melancholy today, pale and distracted. He assured me it was not regret and agreed to see the doctor soon.

7th January

Still no news on J's condition but the change in him is most unsettling.

I have been choosing fabric with Mama and deciding upon my bridesmaids. There is simply too much to do!

Another break in the journal occurred here. I pictured her occupying those days with wedding preparations. But there was something else unfolding.

13th January

Elspeth is so truculent!

I paused over my great grandmother's name. 'Truculent.' This was a different woman to the one I knew. One painted by a sister she had so rarely spoken of. I'd always assumed that was due to the nature of her death. Now, doubt rose up from these pages. And the nature of that sisterhood.

1st February

Elspeth introduced Henry to our house tonight. A fine man of a good family. He is studying art and hopes one day to be a painter. A portraitist, he says. How thrilling! So much more interesting than work at the council but I console myself with the fact that John's job will give us stability. Still, I cannot help but wonder what it would be like to sit for such a portrait. Elspeth is so fortunate and yet she is not grateful. If I had such a strong, devoted fellow, I should not wear a meagre smile.

Her unchecked words were a clear, stark voice in the room as if she stood there with me now. Alive and bristling with self-assurance.

I leafed through many more pages of wedding preparations. Food, fabrics, gifts and guests. It was interminable but the author was clearly enjoying her moment in the sun. It was so mundane that I almost missed that single, bald statement.

14th March

John is ill.

Despite her previous, petulant words, I felt a sudden pang of sympathy for this girl. The wedding she had so embraced seemed in jeopardy. I paused on the thought.

I knew there was no wedding. What was I

thinking? I'd let the reality of what awaited her slip away.

16th March

John has sworn me to secrecy as he does not want anything to prevent him 'doing his duty' if war breaks out. What nonsense he speaks sometimes! Why would this occur to him before the thought that our wedding might be marred by such a pronouncement? Of course, I will not tell a soul.

There were more pages of her thoughts on marriage which, had she not been of marrying age, I would have thought came from the hand of a child. She skimmed over her intended's illness as if it were a minor inconvenience. But a shadow was forming and it grew with each entry.

4th April

We attempted to go to the theatre and John coughed so much we had to leave. This is unbearable! What will happen at our wedding? I have nightmares about our day in church. My wedding forever remembered for his fractured lungs.

I do pity him, of course.

THOSE LAST WORDS were so frighteningly hollow, as if she had to remind herself to care. I read on, already knowing the ending of the tale but no less keen to discover the path that led to it. The next entry reached out from the page.

7th May

Henry came to call today.

A new tone had crept in.

Elspeth was out visiting cousins so I thought it best to take tea with him. He has such a light manner about him. I do wonder why he would choose to be with such a sour woman as my sister.

A string pulled behind my chest, my great grandmother on the other end of it.

30th May

Henry. Tea. Walk. Such a darling day.

The gaps between her entries were becoming longer.

4th June

Henry calls most days now. We walked out by the catacombs again. It is so peaceful there. My spring has been too delightful. John is so taken up by his work that he must be relieved I am kept amused.

28th June

John called with dull details of the shooting of some Archduke. He coughed more than usual but assured me all was in order for our wedding. I cannot bear to think of it now.

The words had found a new urgency. As if they were racing towards the end I knew.

15th July

It is just too much! John called in uniform today! He

says he has volunteered! I asked which army could possibly want him. All he could say was that war was inevitable and he was ready to do his bit for king and country. I did remind him that he had agreed to be loyal to me first of all. He assured me the wedding is not in doubt.

He might just be wrong about that.

A whole new tone had infected the pages now.

17th July

A darling day with Henry out at the catacombs. The heart knows its mind!

18th July

Henry. My dearest love.

4th August

This is unimaginable! There is war! John, my John, my groom, says he must go! Must go! How could he? Our wedding is almost upon us and he is leaving. How can this be? Shame on him.

5th August

Shame on you, Lord Kitchener, for filling John's head with such nonsense. Our country does not need him. I need him to stand next to me in church and take me as his wife. That *is his duty!*

Her words were clinical.

10th August

John has gone. He said he had to, it was his duty and that I shouldn't miss him. I have Henry to console me. He would never leave me for some foolish war.

14th August

I am a widow before I am even a bride.

I stopped, suddenly taking in the full meaning of those words.

I read on with a darkening heart. There were more deaths in this story than the one I had known about.

It is such a waste! The telegram was sent to John's brother. They weren't close and there was no other family. He broke the news with no emotion. John would be laid to rest in some foreign land. He should never have gone and left me. Mother says I should wear mourning. I am in black when I should have been in white. I cannot think how to console myself.

Some of the pages had been torn from the diary here. Not carefully, but with rough, harsh hands. There were no distinguishable words on the scraps that clung to the spine. I turned the pages that remained, backwards then forwards as if something might appear in the space between them.

But the next entry was two words so jarring they seemed almost cruel. I already knew their meaning.

30th August

WEDDING DAY

My wide eyes would not move from those words. But of course there was to be a wedding. Why else would she have been found in the dress? I looked at the newspaper clippings again. The groom had been sent for. The words filled up my mind.

There was so much vibrancy in the next entry that it was easy to forget this wedding would never happen.

The day I never thought would dawn has finally arrived! How marvellous it is to be so loved! Mother balked at the idea of using the same date, same church and dress, but economy must be adhered to. These are war times. It was all booked and paid for, in any event. What a day to cherish this will be. My beloved has already left me flowers this morning with a note telling me to meet him at the usual place. The catacombs. What romance! The place we have spent so many beautiful, loving afternoons. It is not done to see the bride on the wedding morning, but we have not had the most conventional of beginnings. What harm can it do?'

MY HEART STALLED on those last words.

The blank pages of the diary that followed told their own story.

I watched the moon sending an uneven trail of light across the black lawn. How long had I been here lost in a book with no ending?

I looked down at the box again.

Why had Great Grandmother left this for me?

The story had turned like a watch being carefully wound towards that inevitable day. Then nothing. If there was an answer in here, my mind was so shrouded in questions I couldn't find it.

I WOKE in the night midway through dreams of bloodied brides and sealed tombs. Did I catch the glimmer of eyes in the darkness? A blade slicing through satin and flesh? I turned on the bedside light. The box was there on the table beside me.

I breathed out all the nonsense that lives in the dark and let reality slowly leak back in.

Answers. That was the only thing that could end this rhythm of fear. Its noise had been allowed to echo through this city with legends of phantoms and impossible death for too long.

I opened the box again.

The same sepia faces stared out. Blown away by time. But one small clipping fluttered onto my lap. A death notice preserved by some anonymous soul long after the events of this diary.

Henry James Letheridge, aged 65, died 2nd May 1954

Dearly beloved of Millicent Greyling so cruelly taken from him on their wedding day.

I scanned the newspaper reports again with a finer mind, sieving through the details. The engagement notice of Millicent and Henry was there. He'd been Elspeth's before and Millicent took him from her. But she'd clearly set her sights on Henry before that. It was Henry who Millicent was supposed to meet at the catacombs the morning of their wedding.

I stared at all the story laid out on my bed. Clippings, notes, a diary. It began to reassemble. The answer was there. Millicent Greyling had not taken it all to her grave nor had her sister Elspeth. I had to go to the catacombs. The answer lay with the ghosts. I was sure of it.

I WENT ALONE. Anyone else would have told me to wait until it was light. What good could it do now? But I wasn't sure good had anything to do with this.

The moon cast its muted light across the bars to the entrance of the catacombs, sending shadowed stripes across the old stones. Moss and ivy had taken hold, alongside discarded cans and cheap prosecco bottles, the litter of lovers who still met out here. Perhaps Millicent Greyling's ghost and her story inspired some romantic notions alongside the mystery and horror of her death. Her blood-slashed body forever beautiful, never growing old, always waiting for her groom in her white wedding gown.

A snap. I stopped and swung round. The wind turned through the dead leaves and swept them through the bars as if guiding me. I already knew what must be done. I knew what I was looking for. I'd come prepared.

The rusted bars were stiff. The crowbar scraped and ground into the lock. I leant on it with all my weight until the metal finally gave. I stumbled as the bars slowly opened. My eyes remained fixed on the bare stone floor, the scene of my ancestor's murder. A dank smell filled the space. I tried to picture where she might have lain. Had she seen her killer? Was it a stranger or a familiar face reflected on her wide, dying eyes? A lover? A sister? I pushed that thought away.

A cold air breathed up from the vaulted hall beyond. Walls, green-black with mould and algae, glistened with damp as I followed the stone passageway. A one-way path for some.

The first tomb was a grey stone chest by the side of a wall. No crests or grand wording had been carved into it. There was merely one inscription – a blessing, a name and two dates with one dash between them to mark a lifetime. I moved down the dark corridor, further into the catacombs, the blade of my torch sweeping over the floor and walls until it found another of the stone sarcophagi, engraved again with a similar blessing, name and dates. This time I ran a hand along the rough stone and traced my finger through the carving. 'Lord bless this dearly departed soul,' I read.

I stood for a moment, contemplating the words before forging on down the great hall. My footsteps echoed round the vaulted ceiling. The solemn dark had the feel of an abandoned cathedral. But only the dead walked here now. I passed each new tomb until there was only one left. The fifteenth tomb.

I stood before it and waited patiently as though at an altar. I was right. There could be no other explanation. Finally, I set my torch at an angle to shine down on the stone lid and began with the crowbar. At first, it would not budge. I redoubled my efforts, pausing only to take a few breaths. With one final great heft, it shifted. The slab moved slowly aside with a grinding noise. My eyes took a moment to adjust but the light touched what I knew would be there.

I picked up the torch and shone the beam down into the face of the fifteenth soul that lay at rest. Or perhaps not at rest at all. An anonymous soul with no name. No dates and no blessings carved into their tomb.

'Count the blessings,' my great grandmother's note had instructed. Only fourteen bodies were ever laid to rest here. This was the fifteenth, the one who had interred himself after his bloody deed. There had never been any way the murderer could have left the tomb and the key be placed back in his victim's hand. When I had finally accepted that single fact, there was only one possible answer. He did not leave.

He had remained here in these catacombs, ready for his death, holding the knife to his chest with both hands like a knight in his bone fingers. A soldier in his military finery. A borrowed army uniform.

Of course, John William Trenchard was never called upon to serve his country in war due to his ill-health. Millicent had been very clear in her diaries about his pronounced cough. He would never have been someone the army would have welcomed into its ranks. His country did not need him. He served them adequately enough at home, here in England, in Exeter, working for the council in the town hall. A boring job, she'd said, but the same town hall that housed a vault that contained an old key that, once copied, could easily be returned. When the telegram announcing his death had been dispatched by him, he was free and dead to everyone. Dead to the woman he knew had deceived him, betrayed him more than once and would do so again and again. He was dying anyway, why not bury himself with her for eternity? Why cough and choke his way to the end with an adulterous wife when he could be with her forever and in this glorious tomb?

He had to protect his honoured name. To everyone else, he'd be remembered as one of the first to die in the war. Through all the chaos and turmoil of that Great War, like many, he disappeared. No one looked for bodies as proof. There were too many unknown soldiers. Millicent had been so easy to lure out here. What happened when she arrived? The shock of seeing him alive. Had he explained her fate? Had she felt the key to her freedom in her hand? Some things would never be answered.

His last act had to leave an unsolvable question over who killed Millicent. He'd left the key that would provide an impenetrable mystery, one behind which he could forever hide his crime.

But Elspeth Greyling had known enough to leave breadcrumbs. 'Count the blessings.'

Had she known everything? Or merely suspected? Why did she remain silent?

I found no answers staring into that skull's empty sockets. The blade still in his hands. What would happen if the truth was known?

Well, I thought, as I placed the box inside the makeshift tomb and replaced the slab with some effort, perhaps some things are better left a mystery.

———————

VICTORIA DOWD is the award-winning author of the bestselling *Smart Woman's Mystery* series. She has been shortlisted for the CWA Dagger. Her debut novel, *The Smart Woman's Guide to Murder*, won The People's Book Prize for fiction and was In Search of the Classic Mystery Novel's Book of the Year 2020. Her fifth book, *Murder Most Cold*, won the Grand Puzzly award of 2023 and was a finalist in both the Feathered Quill Book Awards and the National Indie Excellence Awards 2024. Victoria was awarded the Gothic Fiction prize for her short fiction. Her work has been published widely in literary journals and anthologies. She also writes the *Adapting Agatha* series where she discusses the various adaptations of Christie novels. She is on the board of the Crime Writers' Association, head of the London Crime Writers' Association, and a judge on the Daggers. She was a defence barrister for many years, working in the Old Bailey. You can find out more about Victoria via the links below:

https://victoriadowd.com

Twitter/X: @victoria_dowd
Instagram: @dowdvictoria
Facebook: @v.dowdauthor

NOTE: *Catacombs* was first published in *Tales of the Gothic – An Anthology of British Horror* from Red Cape Publishing.

A DOLL'S DRESS

ELLEN ALPSTEN

At birth, the nametag on my baby basin was longer than myself: Scheherazade Sarah Smithwick.

'You were so small, you wore this doll's dress,' Pa would say, welling up, holding up a teddy, which was dressed in a frilly frock. Dozens of these cuddly toys adorned his and Mary's bed. The teddy stared at me, beady eyed, as Mary added, 'You would hardly fit in it today, would you?' It's not only in fairy tales that stepmothers can be wicked.

But she had a point. Those days were long gone. My slender sub-teen-self had stretched like a balloon. Even if I had nothing but air in my stomach, I filled out, further and further. There was too much of me; much more than there was ever of Ella, Mary's daughter, my stepsister. 'Shall we drop the "step"?' Ella had suggested at Pa and Mary's wedding. 'We are on par.' Not quite. Slinky Ella won a scholarship to a prized London private school, wearing frumpy flannel skirts at calf-length, while I took the hemline of my state secondary uniform ever higher, taking care to hide the scars in the folds of flesh on my thighs. My skin is the same tawny colour as the couch in the front room, Mary says. You enter it to the right after the entrance door, when facing the stairs. The kitchen, and a small patio, lie beyond.

. . .

'WHAT ARE YOU WEARING TONIGHT THEN?' Mary asked during breakfast.

'Tonight?' My hand hovered, the toast suspended mid-air.

'I asked Ella to take you along to a party,' Pa said. 'Her friend, Pandora, got accepted for St. Martin's.'

Ella, who studied Medicine in her second year at Imperial, gave me a quick smile. I, who folded T-shirts in the pregnancy department of H&M – 'future mums feel all neat with you around' the manager had chirped – felt my mouth drying up. I remembered Posh Pandora, all moonlit skin and flaxen hair; her grey gaze goring me, dissecting our differences. Central St. Martin's! I knew the website by heart, scrolling away, wondering about how to get past those hallowed gates. Heaven was this former granary store close to King's Cross Station, buzzing with genius and housing gods and goddesses in training, who had been good at school and even better at putting a portfolio together. Sometimes, before I fell asleep, I imagined big blobs of paint staining Mary's porch, clay sticking to her Corian kitchen counter, and her skin scored by a stray pin from dressmaking.

The toast went into the bin. I should eat fruit instead, but my life was going pear-shaped as it was.

THE SCENTED WARMTH of Pandora's night garden locked London out. The city's shapes retreated into their grey shell; the air was like a steamed-up looking glass. Dad's old blue overall clung to me at all the wrong places; a floral scarf hid my crazy black curly hair, and my flip-flops slapped my soles. Ella's brown straight mane swished, her little black dress fitting just-so over her pale limbs, as the gravel of the long driveway crunched beneath her shiny high heels. The bell rang, sounding as deep and bronze as the knocker on the tall timber door. Loud music tore the silence apart and sharp stabs of blacklight dotted the blinding white of the stucco pillared entrance. Pandora's brother leant on the door, his smooth chest and his bare feet clashing with his fathers' pin-stripe suit, sleeves and trousers rolled up. He had dropped out of school and trained as a tree surgeon. 'Come on in! It's wicked. Nobody knows anyone. P's still in the studio but shan't be a moment.'

That must be P for pretentious.

Already there were empty glasses and half-eaten plates everywhere. A girl lunged past me – 'Oops, sorry! Wow, love your outfit!' – to seize a fencing mask that hung on the wall. She donned it, shrieking, 'Hit me, ladies!' Two Asian looking girls, wearing intricately patterned vintage Kimonos, open to reveal black lace bras and torn jeans, started shooting Champagne corks at her shielded head, golden foam spluttering over their hands and feet from the bottlenecks. Just then, a feral pack stormed past us, shouting, and singing, bearing a young man on a chair. Helpless with laughter, he almost slipped from his shaky throne but hung on to his kippah, pressing the skullcap to the back of head.

'What's happening?' Ella asked.

'We are playing at Jewish Wedding,' he cheered, before being flung against the mattresses of Pandora's parents' bed, which were propped up against the wall. Rolling off, he still kept hold of his kippah, but scrambled between two girls and a boy, who had just lost his trousers in a game of strip-poker. He sat in his boxers, which were embroidered with tiny butterflies. I heard shouts – 'Kiss! Kiss! Kiss!' – and the guys gave in, making the kippah slip after all.

'Where's Pandora?' Ella asked. 'I haven't seen her since school finished a year ago.'

The tree-trimming pinstripe-suited youth

hesitated. 'Ah,' he said. 'Yes, P was – busy. Come. The studio is in the stables.'

We should see Pandora's art: surely some searingly serene, smooth stone structures, whose meaning was left entirely to the imagination.

THE STUDIO WAS A WHITE, small house hidden away behind the white, large house – like that toy; a doll hiding another doll. As we entered, organ music thundered and countless candles bathed the long room in a soft glow. At the far end, a young man chiselled at what looked like a sugarloaf. Faded jeans hung on his snake-like hips and a threadbare pale-pink shirt covered broad shoulders and sculpted arms. His nervy hands chipped away; clouds of candied crystals rose. He frowned with concentration; his shoulder-length blond hair tied in a ponytail, the nape of his neck shaven. He turned and his classic profile made me catch my breath; he looked like one of the statues I had secretly admired when my class visited the British Museum. Secretly, because the rest of my class just made fun of their short willies and rigid faces. P laughed and poured a full bottle of Smirnoff over the sculpted sweet, setting it alight. He shouted, 'Watch out!' Flames shot up and we ducked for cover. As we peered out from behind the faded-velvet couch, the last of turquoise and veridian plunged about, before all glow ceded. It smelt of fudge.

'Why did you do that?' I asked.

'Why?' He seemed surprised.

'Yes. That's what I always want to ask about art …'

'To show the stark seasons in Russia, and the opposites in the Slavic soul? Or, possibly, to symbolise the thirst of the sweet for the savoury. Or does it express the ephemerous essence of human life? But you ask the right question …'

'Do I?' Something in me popped. My insides turned fluid and foaming, like the champagne bottle earlier on. The whole world fizzed. At home, I had learned to keep my head down to duck and dive from Mary's sniping comments. In school, I was derided for being a swot when I wanted to know more. I had neither thought that there was somewhere where questions were welcome, nor that someone might think them 'right'. It feels like ants marching in my veins; making me smile, as if tickled.

'Yes. Art is like life. It is not about the who, what, where or when. It's about the why.' Long dark lashes framed his light-grey eyes.

'Where's Pandora?' Ella's voice flickered. She

had grown so pale – I caressed her naked upper arm. This is something that does not fit so easily within the straight frames of her world. Sometimes it is good to take a step back to see the bigger picture. She casts me a grateful glance while she struggles for balance.

There was a moment of silence.

'I am called P now,' he gently rebuked her.

P's younger brother flung himself on the couch. 'Does anyone know a cocktail recipe mixed with burnt sugar?'

P laughed, and then looked at us. 'There's also something that *I* always wanted to ask.'

'Yes?' The colour in Ella's cheeks rose. P or Pandora, she liked them just as much. And I could clearly see why; even if their shape was still crystallising, it already sparkled more than ever.

'Would you model for me?'

'Well—' she started, smoothing her little black dress.

'No, no. You,' P said, his gaze a beam of light that set me on fire.

COME DAWN, I returned home, tiptoeing into Pa and Mary's bedroom. Then I set to work in the kitchen. When Ella joined me, puffy-eyed and hedgehog-haired, she stood and stared. 'What is that?'

I stepped back, considering. 'My first piece of art.'

If P had taught me that there are right questions, I had grown to taking the right actions. And it had been such fun setting to work, freeing myself. The shredded doll's dress lay piled up, drenched in ketchup, and skewered by the tip of a long, sharp knife.

Ella looked at it for a long time, all silent. Then, a small smile showed on her face and she nodded. 'It's marvellous. How will you name it?'

I hesitated, thinking, and then welling up. 'It's called, *In your end lies my beginning.*'

'That's a great title. Let's do just that. And may I please come along on the trip?' my sister said, slinging her arm around my shoulder.

ELLEN ALPSTEN WAS BORN and raised in the Kenyan highlands, where she dressed up their many pets (cats, dogs, chicken, geese, a stroppy Polo pony, a wounded Serval cat and at times a baby crocodile) and forced them to listen to her stories. After her very mediocre A-levels, Ellen studied at the 'Institut d'Etudes Politiques de Paris', where she won the Grande Ecole's short story competition with her novella, *Meeting Mr. Gandhi*. Following her MSc in PPE, she worked as a News-Anchor for Bloomberg TV London, doing gruesome night shifts on breakfast TV. Today, she is an author, an international journalist and a Creative Writing Lecturer at St. Mary's University. Her debut novel, *Tsarina,* and its sequel, *The Tsarina's Daughter*, were widely translated and shortlisted for numerous awards. Ellen's next historical fiction series, *The Last Princess,* is out in autumn 2024. You can find out more about Ellen via the links below:

https://www.ellenalpsten.com
Twitter/X: @EAlpsten_Author
Instagram: @ellenalpsten_author

THE CASE OF THE
ASS'S HEAD

PENNY BATCHELOR

'F airies, will you stop hitting each other. Bottom, you're not in your costume and can someone *please* tell me where Titania is?'

Mrs Ashbourne was a widow of a certain age, known in the small English town for her calmness in a crisis, her large embonpoint never heaving into hysterics and her hair, the exact colour match of her Russian Blue cat's fur, staying firmly in its pinned curls even when Hitler forced her to crawl under a table during a visit to her sister in the Blitz.

Today, however, in the backdrop of the ruins the quaint English town was famous for, a quarter of an hour before the evening's production of *A Midsummer Night's Dream* was due to take place, her composure was showing unprecedented signs of straining at the seams, for she was the local amateur dramatics society's current director under very trying circumstances.

Eugenia Porter, known to her three closest friends as Gene, surveyed the scene before her, a pair of tortoiseshell sunglasses shading her eyes from the still powerful rays that bathed the spartan set in a joyful glow. *Looking on the bright side, at least it's not raining*, she thought, hoping that the clear blue sky would remain untroubled by the one grey cloud up above.

Her prompt's chair was situated at the right-hand side of the stage, the well-thumbed play script lay on her knee, and on the back of her seat, as usual, rested her two walking sticks.

In five minutes' time the paying guests, whose ticket fees were to go towards raising money for the nearby hospital's children's ward, would be free to enter the makeshift auditorium, but the cast were nowhere near ready. Squinting, Gene could see her mother, Mrs Porter, directing her minions at the refreshments table, a solely managerial rather than hands-on role she had reluctantly taken to show willing. Acting in a theatre production, in her learned opinion, was best left to schoolchildren or the professionals, to avoid starstruck amateurs making a spectacular show of themselves rather than the playwright's manuscript.

'Now, children, stand up straight and behave as if you are fairies and nymphs like I told you,' instructed Edith, local schoolteacher and Gene's best friend, expeditiously breaking up two boys attempting an impromptu wrestling match, and removing the crafted ass's head from a hard to catch nymph who ran in front of the stage braying 'hee-haw'. Some of her seven-year-olds had been co-opted to play what Mrs Ashbourne had envisaged as angelic fairy folk but, even though the brood were dressed in green shorts or dresses and bedecked with flowers, their behaviour was more akin to that hailing from hellfire rather than the celestial city.

'Leads, gather round, only five minutes to go!' Mrs Ashbourne rallied her troops into battle. Gene watched on, willing them all to give it their best shot, especially her other two best friends: Joey, her late brother's constant companion who was now a police constable conscripted to play one of the rude mechanicals; and Mary, a solicitor's wife who had moved to the town with her husband a few years previously, taking the role of Hermia. This evening, however, Mary was conspicuous by her absence.

Finally, dressed in his Bottom costume, Colonel Hargreaves ambled up to the director, joining Mary's slightly jittery-looking husband, Peter, as Lysander; the grocer's twenty-year old daughter Caroline radiantly playing Helena; and mature George Franklin, whose casting as dashing young Demetrius stretched the imagination of even elderly Mrs Wiseman who was renowned for going out without her spectacles. He'd been the only volunteer for the part.

'Where on earth is Hermia?' asked Mrs Ashbourne, fanning away her rising perspiration with the programme especially printed by the local newspaper for the event. Peter's eyes anxiously scoured the scene, his shoulders relaxing when he spotted his wife, wearing a beautiful shimmering gold dress, running up to the group as quickly as her heeled shoes could allow her. Mary usually was strictly a flat lace ups or Wellington Boots type of woman.

'Sorry, sorry,' she said, offering no explanation for her absence. Peter took her hand in his and squeezed it encouragingly.

A steely glint in Mrs Ashbourne's eye betrayed her burgeoning exasperation. 'Company, it's about time to let in one's audience. Remember to speak up, look at Eugenia if you forget your lines and, most importantly, enjoy yourself. Break a leg!' then adding, 'Well, please try not to but you know what I mean.'

With that she nodded to post office cashier, Miss Taylor, whose job it was to take the ticket money and keep the impatient hoards at bay. Two large velvet curtains hid the stage from view. Behind them hung a painted backdrop, concealing the actors who awaited their cue to enter, although Eugenia did wonder why an artist had gone to all that effort when at the rear was delightful real-life scenery consisting of the castle's moss-speckled ruins overhung by centuries' old oak trees.

Miss Taylor unclipped the rope barrier that

marked the separation between the auditorium and the locals congregating in the rest of field and declared the production officially open. First in, their rank and benevolence entitling them to front seats with padded cushions rather than an ordinary deckchair usually reserved for cricket match spectators, were Lord and Lady Abney, who had graciously supplied the venue, which was part of their private back garden.

Next came Major Moore, dressed in a suit and tie despite the summer temperature, muttering loudly that the casting of Colonel Hargreaves as Bottom was perfection because he was an old fool. Gene was well aware of the two men's longstanding feud over a bravery medal Colonel Hargreaves was awarded after the Second World War, with Major Moore, whose regalia did not include the aforementioned gong, insisting that Hargreaves was as courageous as a dead mouse and had lied about his heroics. She briefly pondered whether to go up to him and change the subject, for his reverberant voice travelled far in the open air and the actors could probably hear him behind the curtain but, by the time she grasped her walking sticks and raised herself to her feet, the major's wife had sensibly brought him a cup of tea and a scone, which gave his mouth something else to do rather than slander.

Many others followed, a number making a beeline for the deckchairs further back. Some came prepared with picnic blankets to sit on, flasks of tea and tins replete with home-made cakes, and received a disapproving look from Gene's mother, who saw the action of bringing refreshments rather than paying for them as akin to snatching toys out of the hands of suffering children.

This performance was a big occasion for the townsfolk. It was not just a chance to avail themselves of culture, but also a rare opportunity to see the castle ruins up close, an action usually prohibited by the Land Registry.

Gene's hands trembled when the moment they'd all been waiting for came and the stage curtains opened to enthusiastic applause. Theseus strode onto the stage saying the words 'Now, fair Hippolyta, our nuptial hour draws on apace.' Minutes passed quickly as Gene intricately followed the dialogue with her script, mouthing lines to the odd cast member who feigned an artistic pause whilst frantically trying to remember what followed. She beamed with pleasure when Joey said all his lines correctly, thanks, she was in no doubt, to the hours they'd spent practising them to perfection.

Act Two ended with Hermia exiting the stage. A short interval provided an opportunity for the audience to purchase more tea and cake, then the play continued. Colonel Hargreaves' appearance sporting an ass's head elicited much mirth from the audience, prompting Major Moore to shout out 'Bravo!' and strike his hands together repeatedly until his wife deftly took one in hers. Gene shivered involuntarily, a feeling of anxiety sweeping over her as the one grey cloud in the sky briefly drifted in front of the sun. For Mrs Ashbourne's sake, she didn't want the Colonel to be put off his stride. Her concern grew when Mary dashed onto the stage thirty seconds after her cue, causing Demetrius to repeat his line 'O, why rebuke you him that loves you so? Lay breath so bitter on your bitter foe.'

'Whatever can be the problem with Mary?' Gene wondered, for she usually was as punctual as the speaking clock.

Indeed, something was amiss with Gene's friend. Mary's flushed cheeks were the colour of ladybirds and she stumbled over her words, turning to Gene for help with a line. Gene mouthed the sentence and willed her friend to do well.

The action continued through Act Three and soon it was Act Four, with its comic scene involving Titania and Bottom laying down to sleep. As Theseus and Hippolyta subsequently exchanged their lines, out of the corner of her eye Gene saw

Bottom's leg spasm. He kicked Titania, who cried 'Ow' and then tried to mask her exclamation by turning it into a loud snore. Bottom's body began to convulse violently.

'Looks like he's having A Midsummer Night's *Bad* Dream,' laughed Major Moore, slapping his knee jollily. Theseus and Hippolyta turned and looked at Bottom, then at Gene, wondering whether the Colonel was embracing a form of method acting, currently popular across the Atlantic, or if they should stop the play. Bottom's hands reached for the ass's head and tried to pull it off but then, with one shuddering spasm, he grew still.

'Is there a doctor here?' Gene called out to the open-mouthed audience. Peter rushed to the supine body. PC Hardcastle leapt onto the stage from behind the backdrop and helped Peter pull off the stricken man's ass's head. Both men would forever remember the visage that faced them. The Colonel's raised brows topped eyes wide open in fear, his lips were contorted into a sardonic grin and drool rolled a sticky trail down his chin. Neither man could find a pulse.

Jocy turned to Peter and uttered two dreaded words.

'He's dead.'

. . .

THIRTY MINUTES LATER, Gene, now using her wheelchair, was in deep conversation with Joey in the impromptu interview area created behind the stage, away from beady eyes. The cast, along with the audience who had been told to stay until they had given their names and addresses to the quickly summoned Inspector Shields who had robustly taken control, were in shock, discussing how such a thing could have happened in their town and what a fine man Colonel Hargreaves was. Major Moore's lips remained closed on the latter topic.

Gene, being a sensible young woman, had swiftly asked her mother to organise complimentary refreshments for the crowd, including a stiff brandy from her father's flask for a stunned Mrs Ashbourne.

'Does Dr Roberts know if the Colonel died of natural causes or was killed?' she asked her friend. Joey made eye contact with her for a second too long, before scrutinising the grass and refraining to place his hand on her arm, a gesture he had the overwhelming urge to carry out. He knew Gene was an avid reader of murder stories, but reading about a dead body in a novel and seeing one next to you was quite a different thing entirely.

'Dr Roberts is of the opinion that he was poisoned. Strychnine, probably. Looks like the killer sprinkled powder into the ass's head. Colonel Hargreaves will have inhaled it when he put it on. Strychnine can take a while to do its worst.'

Thankfully the local GP had been in the audience and was quick to help.

'Crikey. I wonder why the Colonel didn't take the costume head off when he began to feel ill?'

'Who knows,' replied Joey, 'perhaps he was a trouper and didn't want to interrupt the performance. Would you want to get on the wrong side of Mrs Ashbourne?'

'Quite.' A worrying thought then hit Gene. 'Gosh, what about the little girl who I saw running about with the ass's head on before the play? Margaret, wasn't it? How is she?'

Joey exhaled with relief. To onlookers he looked rather incongruous doing police work whilst still dressed in a ragged workman costume. 'Dr Roberts examined her and said she's fine. He's sent her home to bed with a sleeping draught and strict instructions for her mother to keep an eye on her overnight.'

The sun's rays had weakened now, and two more grey clouds littered the sky. Gene placed her thin, knitted cardigan over her shoulders in thought. 'Does Inspector Shields have a suspect yet?'

'No,' replied Joey. 'He's busy organising the coroner and interviewing the audience, something I need to join him with. I say, Gene, would you mind asking the cast if they noticed anything suspicious before we get to it officially? They are more likely to open up to you.' Joey held Gene, the sister of his childhood best friend Johnny, who was killed in the last month of the war, in very high esteem, higher than she was yet to realise.

'Of course, anything to help.'

With that, Joey went off to continue his official police business; whispers about murder spread amongst the gathering, and Gene called out to a frazzled Edith, who had just finished reuniting the child actors with their parents. Most of the children were reduced to tears by the earlier event, apart from one red-headed boy who declared it was the most exciting thing that had ever happened to him.

'What a dreadful evening,' said Edith as she sat down on the chair next to her old friend. Edith had been briefly engaged to Johnny before his death terminated that arrangement, and the two women had leaned on each other since.

'How are you?' Gene asked.

'Shocked. Same as everyone, I suppose. Poor

Colonel. What a way to go. Who on earth would have done such a thing?'

'Who indeed. We know that the major was not a fan of his, but he was in the front row the whole time. Dr Roberts apparently said the major was poisoned with strychnine powder; he thinks the killer placed it in the costume ass's head. It looks like the powder was put in the head *during* the performance because young Margaret tried it on just before the play began and the doctor says she hasn't any symptoms.' Gene leaned towards her friend and lowered her voice.

'Did you notice anything strange? Where were the costumes kept during the play?'

Edith clasped her arms around her whilst she cast her mind back. It had been a long day. 'There's a large shed behind the backdrop for the actors to change in. It can fit about four people in at one time – the women and men took it in turns. Props are kept there too. The children arrived in their costumes. Simpler that way, I thought, no chance of them losing clothes. None of them had to change costume during the play.'

'Where were you during the performance?' Gene asked.

'I was behind the backdrop, organising the children, keeping them quiet and telling them when it was their turn to go on stage. Not an easy job.'

'Did you see anyone go into the shed?'

Creases appeared on Edith's forehead. 'Well, the Colonel had to go to the shed and change before Act Three. I noticed Mary go in there. A couple of the children did too – they were bored between scenes and wanted to see what was inside. I wasn't backstage during all the interval though, I had to organise lavatory visits and orange squash for the children.'

'Thank you.'

'Quite the detective, aren't you, Gene?' smiled Edith.

'Just helping PC Hardcastle,' Gene replied.

Her next interviewee was George Franklin, who had put on a brown overcoat over his costume. A small silver hip flask stuck out of the left-hand side pocket. He unscrewed the top and took a swig.

'Whisky. Medicinal,' he explained, then delved into the other pocket for a handkerchief, causing an England's Glory matchbox to fall out. He swiftly put it back then wiped his damp forehead with the handkerchief. 'Damned rotten business. Could do with a cigarette. Run out of matches and forgot to bring my cigarette case anyway.'

Gene wrinkled her nose. The entrenched smell

of tobacco emanating from his coat disagreed with her. She had always wondered why anyone would find the habit remotely appealing.

'It's a great shock. Poor Colonel. Do you know of anyone who might have wanted to harm him?'

George shrugged his shoulders and availed himself of another tot of whisky, the evening light reflecting off the metal flask. 'We all know that he and the major had no time for each other. The major's been saying for years that the Colonel faked his war record and received his gallantry medal under false pretences. I saw them come to blows over it once.'

'Did you see anything odd today?' asked Gene. 'Anyone being where they shouldn't?' She noticed that there was an orange smear on George's forehead where he had wiped it with his handkerchief. Stage make-up, she concluded. It would take a lot more than that for people to suspend their disbelief at him playing a character supposed to be more than half his age.

'I saw Mrs Ashbourne crack a smile,' George joked. Gene sighed inwardly, thinking it was going to be a long night.

'Nothing else?'

'Mary kept disappearing and she was late on cue. I saw a couple of the fairy children go into the shed. That's all. If you'll excuse me, I must go and check on Caroline. She's most distressed.' He turned to leave, then, a pace away, turned back.

'There was one other thing. In the interval, I saw the major go behind the stage. I asked him what he was doing, and he said he was stretching his legs.'

Gene needed to stretch her legs herself, for a prolonged and troubled early entry into this world had affected her muscles and mobility. She reached for her walking sticks, her treasured pair with carved birds' heads on that her cousin had made for her thirtieth birthday the previous year, and got to her feet, heading for Mary, who had been very hard to locate, despite the inspector's ban on the cast and audience leaving.

'Mary!' she called, walking towards the steps at the side of the stage where she spotted her friend sitting next to Peter. Mary had changed out of her costume and was now back in her usual attire of a plain dress belted at the waist, topped by a cardigan.

The pair smiled and made space for Gene to sit by them. She couldn't help but notice that Mary still looked rather red in the cheeks, and it wasn't a shade caused by healthy sunshine.

'How are you, Eugenia? Frightful business,' said Peter.

'I'm well, thank you. You acted admirably, rushing to help the Colonel.'

Peter started to look rather green around the gills. 'I spent the war training troops in Catterick. Dicky ticker. Never seen a dead body before.'

'Are you well, Mary?' Gene asked her friend. 'You seemed to disappear rather a lot this evening.'

Mary looked round to see if anyone could overhear the trio. It was unlikely because the nearest group to them were engaged in noisy speculation.

'I have been rather under the weather these past few days,' she said. Peter put his arm round his wife. 'I thought you've been quieter than usual but put it down to nerves. Are you coming down with something darling?' he asked.

Mary took her husband's hand in hers. 'My love, I think I've *already* come down with something. I've been feeling very nauseous and have had to keep rushing to the lavatory. I suspect an addition to our family may be on the way,' she added, smiling nervously.

A delighted Gene, who knew that her friends had long wished to have a child, looked politely aside whilst the pair embraced and Peter expressed his joy. She then congratulated them both, adding, 'So, that's why you kept rushing off! I couldn't be happier for the both of you. I shall look forward to being an honorary aunt and spoiling the little one wretchedly.'

'I'm sure you'll be a marvellous aunt. Please keep it to yourself for the moment though until I've seen Dr Roberts and it's confirmed,' Mary added.

'Of course. May I inquire, when you were going to and fro, did you see anything suspicious?'

'I wasn't taking a lot of notice,' replied Mary. 'I saw a couple of children playing around. In the interval, I went to the back of the field for some privacy because I felt very queasy and I saw Major Moore go behind the backdrop. He exchanged a few words with the Colonel, who turned his back on him and walked off. Poor man, is it true he was poisoned?'

'Yes, Dr Roberts thinks so,' affirmed Gene. 'Most likely strychnine. It's as easy to get hold of as rat poison.'

Peter butted in. 'Mrs Ashbourne told me the other day that she's having terrible problems with rats in her cellar. She thought she'd poisoned them all but then another lot showed up, leaving droppings everywhere.'

'Surely Mrs Ashbourne can't be the killer. She's

more likely to have hit the Colonel round the head with her handbag!' laughed Mary, before realising the inappropriateness of her humour. 'Sorry, poor taste.'

Gene smiled reassuringly at her friend. 'Mrs Ashbourne was near me all the way through the play watching the production, apart from during the interval when she went backstage to talk to the cast.'

'I saw the major in a foul mood when he took his seat after the interval,' said Peter. 'Perhaps he was angry that the Colonel was doing well in the play. Their feud seems to go far back. He came into the practice two weeks ago asking for legal advice on challenging the Colonel's war record. Said he had evidence that the Colonel didn't do the heroic act that he was awarded a medal for.'

'Really?' said Mary, surprised at the cases her husband came across in his professional life beyond conveyancing and writing wills.

'Yes. Roger told him we couldn't help. That's not our line of work. Besides, I don't want to get involved with local disputes if I can help it. George Franklin has been in too asking about claiming a neighbour's land. He said that deeds showed it was really his, but he was on thin legal ground, much to his disgruntlement. I didn't want to touch it with a bargepole; a case we would most likely lose.'

'Which adjacent land was George wanting? To the rear or to the side?'

'Rear. But keep that under your hat,' Peter confided.

'Interesting,' Gene replied. 'Now I'd like to talk to Major Moore. Peter, could you please fetch my wheelchair?'

Peter did just that and pushed Gene to the front of the stage where the major was conversing with neighbours, like the affable gentleman he'd always appeared to be to her. It was only the Colonel who seemed to incense him.

'Eugenia, what a horrid evening,' he said, moving on to the statutory social questions about her health.

'I'm quite well, thank you, despite this evening's events. The poor Colonel. I gather you didn't see eye to eye?' she slyly enquired.

The major had the grace to look slightly, just slightly, repentant. 'Can't say I liked the fellow, a damned liar, but murder? No, he didn't deserve that.'

Gene remembered the major goading the Colonel at the start of the play, and Mary telling her he had approached his nemesis during the interval.

'If you don't mind me asking, Major, I know the subject is rather delicate, but you were seen talking to the Colonel during the interval. May I ask what was discussed?'

The major let out a deep, deflating breath. 'I rather wish I hadn't now. I told Hargreaves last week that I'd found a witness who swore that he'd taken credit for a dead man's heroics. The Colonel said that if I told anyone he'd sue me for libel. I went backstage to tell him that, suing be damned, I was going to the authorities with my evidence. He laughed and walked off, saying he'd be pleased to see the case bankrupt me.'

Gene's eyebrows raised at the prolonged hostility between two grown men who had fought on the same side in the war. If they were in Edith's class, she'd have swiftly dealt with them via detention instead of football practice and a few choice words about how they had let her down badly.

'I see. Did you notice anyone else backstage during the interval?'

'The cast were there. I congratulated Caroline on her marvellous performance. I leant her my handkerchief; she was trying to wipe off a stain on her hand from the shed's handle. She'd gone to have a quiet moment to herself but she said the door was stuck – must have been someone in there getting changed.'

'Do you still have the handkerchief? May I borrow it, please?' Gene asked.

'Of course. It's a very upsetting night, particularly for the ladies with their tender hearts. Keep it for as long as you need, Eugenia.'

The major passed the handkerchief to her. She took a quick look then, holding it by a miniscule area of cloth at the end, promptly locked it away in her handbag.

Behind them a loud voice prevented further conversation. It was Inspector Shields. 'Ladies and Gentlemen, thank you for your patience. PC Hardcastle and I have completed our preliminary enquiries. You're now all free to go home. As a precaution, I suggest that you walk in pairs. We'll be conducting more interviews tomorrow but, in the meantime, if you think of anything that may help our investigation, no matter how small, please contact the station. Thank you.'

Mr and Mrs Porter rushed over to Gene. Joey followed a few paces behind, trying to catch her eye.

'I think we're all ready for our beds,' said John Porter, placing a comforting hand on his daughter's shoulder.

'It's certainly been a day to remember,' Gene replied. An avid reader of detective novels, she'd wisely kept it to herself that the excitement of coming across a real-life case had rendered her wide awake. 'I'd like a word with PC Hardcastle before I leave, if you don't mind.'

The older man turned to the younger. 'Bring her home when you're ready, please, Joseph. Not too late now. I'll see you tomorrow, dear girl.' He leaned down and kissed Gene on the top of her head, then linked his arm in his wife's to depart.

'Joey, there's one person I think you shouldn't let leave,' confided Gene. He knelt on the grass beside her, and she whispered a name into his ear. His eyes opened as wide as they could possibly stretch.

Jumping to his feet he called 'Inspector Shields!' and the long arm of the law sprang into motion.

THE NIGHT WAS AS STILL as the Colonel in the morgue when Joey pushed Eugenia back to her parents' comfortable villa. They passed centuries-old terraced cottages and ventured towards the newer, wider residential streets. Curtains were closed, with the occasional light peeking through between a small textile gap. The town's people were safely in their beds, a matter of great relief to Joey. He'd seen death in the war, but never during the subsequent peace. Until today.

'It won't be too long before we get the results from the police chemist proving the suspect's guilt, thanks to you, Gene. However did you work it out?'

Looking down at the top of her head, which was now clad in a jolly, knitted beret covering her light brown waves, Joey was in awe of his friend. It wasn't the first time she'd solved a case before he did. As children, she always did beat him at jigsaw puzzles.

'You asked me to talk to people and then it all fell together,' she replied. Gene didn't temper the satisfied smile that crossed her face because she knew that Joey, behind her, was unable to see it.

'At first the finger seemed to point at the major and his feud with the Colonel. Mary and Peter saw them behind the stage arguing during the interval. Everyone's whereabouts during the interval was important. We know that the killer sprinkled the strychnine in the costume ass's head either sometime during the first two acts or in the interval, because earlier Margaret put it on and she was absolutely fine.'

They turned a corner, past a huge buddleia in bloom, savouring the simple midsummer pleasure of its honey-like scent.

'From my prompt's chair, I could see the whole audience during the performance and no one left. The major was the only non-cast member spotted behind the stage in the interval. Nobody told me they saw anything else untoward. The ass's head was kept in the shed at the back of the stage where the props were stored, along with costumes for the few actors who needed to change in the middle of the play.'

'If it wasn't the major, it must have been one of the actors or stagehands,' Joey agreed.

'Exactly. But why would anyone want to kill the Colonel in the first place? The Am Dram Players, from what I could see during rehearsals, all rubbed along together well. Then a comment from Peter set me thinking of a possible motive. After I'd spoken to the major, I was as near as certain as I could be of what took place.'

Gene breathlessly continued her explanation. 'George Franklin's house is behind the Colonel's. He thought that some of the land currently part of Colonel Hargreaves' garden was really, according to the deeds, his. The Colonel angrily disagreed, and Peter thought that George's legal case was not strong. It's prime land, which developers would pay a lot of money for to build new houses on.'

'At Mrs Ashbourne's house one day during a read-through, George Franklin went to her basement and took some strychnine she'd bought to kill her rat infestation, or perhaps he simply procured some of his own. At the beginning of this evening's interval he went into the shed when no one else was there, jammed the door for a moment or two, and quickly poured the strychnine powder into the ass's head. Caroline, playing Helena, had tried to go into the shed at that time but found the door locked. She was then approached by the major who, following his stand-off with the Colonel, praised her and lent her his handkerchief. She wanted to use it to clean the orange stain from her hand that she'd acquired from touching the shed door handle.

The pair were a few houses away from the Porters' front door now. Joey slowed his pace, keen to hear the rest.

'The handkerchief and the matchbox, our two pieces of evidence,' he marvelled.

'Yes. George Franklin wore orange make up to try and give him a more youthful appearance, befitting the part of Demetrius. This evening was warm and, no doubt exacerbated by the stress of carrying out his plan, he sweated. I noticed his face was patchy where he'd wiped it. He must have done so with his hand and, without realising, transferred the makeup to the shed door handle when he opened it. I thought it rather odd that he had an empty matchbox in his coat pocket but no cigarettes. Wouldn't a regular smoker have both? And a matchbox is a very handy container in which to transport poison. His coat remained hung up in the shed throughout the play until he retrieved it afterwards. The temperature when I spoke to him was a little mild, but not chilly enough to require him to wear his coat.'

'He didn't want to leave the evidence in the shed for when we came looking. If you hadn't told me to take Franklin in for questioning, I'm sure the first thing he would have done when he left was dispose of the matchbox,' concurred Joey.

They arrived outside the Porters' large, blue front door trailed decoratively with delicate honeysuckle. Gene's father had left it unlocked. Joey opened the door slowly, trying to avoid its customary unpredictable squeak waking the house. He wheeled Gene silently up the front step and into the entrance. Bathed in the soft amber glow of the hall lamp, she placed her sticks on the floor, raised herself to a standing position and faced Joey.

Their eyes were almost on the same level, what with Joey only being a couple of inches taller than his childhood friend. 'I suppose George must have thought that with the Colonel, a single man with no children, being dead, it would be easy for him to claim the land he thought was his,' Gene whispered.

'Greed, one of the three classic motives for murder,' said Joey, his face close to Gene's. 'Along with revenge. And love.'

For once, Gene's usually overflowing mind went totally blank. Although the grandfather clock by the wall kept ticking, it struck her that time, for a second, had stood still.

'There you are, my dear. Do hurry, I left you a cocoa by your bed.'

The pair turned abruptly to see Mrs Porter, enveloped from neck to ankle in an ethereal rose-print robe, descending the stairs.

'I simply couldn't sleep until you came home, not with a murderer at large. Thank you, Joseph, for bringing my daughter home safely. Make sure you're on guard walking home. I take it you are armed with your truncheon?' she enquired.

'No, I'm not in uniform,' replied a flustered Joey.

'Would you like to take John's cricket bat with you?'

'I don't think that will be necessary, Mrs Porter, but thank you for the kind offer.' With that, Joey wished both women a good night and left, closing the door behind him with a gentle yet satisfying clunk.

Upstairs, the tepid cup of cocoa on Gene's bedside table was still delicious but it didn't have the desired soporific effects, for it was hours later before her eyelids finally closed.

Being the prompt for the amateur dramatic society had been fun, she mused as she eventually dozed off, but she'd far rather solve actual mysteries than follow someone else's script.

***

PENNY BATCHELOR is the Amazon-bestselling author of three psychological thrillers: *My Perfect Sister*, *Her New Best Friend* and *The Reunion Party*, all published by Embla Books. A fourth is coming soon. She is a co-founder and judge of the ADCI Literary Prize for adult fiction by a disabled/chronically ill novelist, a columnist for *The Bookseller* and speaks regularly at literary festivals. You can find Penny via the links below:

www.pennybatchelor.co.uk

https://www.amazon.co.uk/stores/Penny-Batchelor/author/B084KZVHGY

Twitter/X: @penny_author

Facebook: @pennyauthor

Instagram: @pennybatchelorauthor

Threads: @pennybatchelorauthor

A THEORY OF EVERYONE

TOM BENJAMIN

I t was the morning Albert Einstein's wife left him. 'It's not as if you'll know the difference,' Mileva glared at her twenty-four-year-old husband through bruised eyes, babe still suckling her breast.

'How can you say that?' he wailed. 'Everything I do, I do for you!'

'Tell that to the boys at the Olympia,' she shot back and went to pack her things. Albert had to admit he had returned late from his discussion club the previous night, but they had become caught up in a discussion over Henri Poincaré's claim that absolute truth is unattainable in Science (Maurice, the philosopher, argued nay, Albert, the theoretical physicist, yea) and time … well, time …

'Herr Doktor is looking a little tired this morning,' commented Freddy, proprietor of Lucky Freddy's, where Albert habitually popped for his *Kafi-crème* and slice of *Rüeblitorte* – carrot cake – before beginning his day at the nearby Federal Institute of Intellectual Property.

'The responsibilities of fatherhood, Freddy,' he replied.

'Ah yes, Herr Doktor. The father bears a heavy burden upon his shoulders.'

'Indeed he does, Freddy,' said Albert. 'You know, this cake really is exceptional.'

'My wife's recipe, Herr Doktor.'

'Albert.'

Albert jumped. Had Mileva had a change of heart? But it was Elsa. 'My goodness, cousin!' They embraced and kissed on both cheeks.

'My darling, how are you? What are you doing here?' Elsa Löwenthal, nee Einstein, was Albert's maternal first cousin, and their fathers were also first cousins, hence her maiden name.

She explained she had been taking the waters at a sanatorium by the Bielersee and stopped in Bern on her way back to Stuttgart. She had called at his apartment that morning but Mileva had explained he had already left for work. 'She hadn't time to chat,' she said. 'She was going to her parents. Is everything well between you two?'

'Quite well, thank you, cousin.'

'Look at you, *meine kleine schildkröte*,' – Elsa had always called Albert her 'little tortoise', which he wasn't sure he approved of as it inferred 'plodding', but Elsa, who was not from the intellectual wing of the family, assured him it was a term of endearment *because of how when we were small your little head would peep from under the blanket* – 'you seem all washed-out, what has the blue stocking been feeding you?'

'Ach,' said Albert, brushing back his hair, which was unruly even then. 'You know, Millie does her best.'

'I always said you needed a good hausfrau, not a woman with her head buried in books.'

Albert experienced a flare of indignation on behalf of his wife, who had come second only to him at the Polytechnic, and Elsa sensed she had gone too far. She smoothed his moustache and pinched his cheek. 'It's a failing of mine – you know you're *meine kleine schildkröte*.'

Albert's eyes welled. He wanted to be back under the blankets in the candlelight when all that mattered was his tricks with numbers and his cousin leaning forward to kiss him on the nose. Before he understood we were grounded in soil, and it was soil to which we would return, like his *liebling*, doll-like Lieserl, whom he and Mileva had lost to the fever and laid to rest the previous year.

'My dear,' said Albert. 'Take a seat. You must try some of Fraù Gründer's delectable *Rüeblitorte*.'

FINDING himself unexpectedly alone in Bern, Albert came to appreciate that it was one thing to work late at the office to avoid the distractions of a crying baby and scornful wife, quite another when it meant an apartment filled by their absence. Sundays were the worst. As a secular Jew, he did not even have the distraction of church. He attempted to work on his papers at the dining table but, in the silence of those Swiss afternoons, the gloom of the second-floor apartment on Kramgasse 49 without Mileva seated beside him – challenging, cajoling, double-checking – Lieserl's phantom laughter would interrupt the scratch of his pen, while the chime from the nearby Zytglogge, the city's ancient city clock, became a funereal toll.

He took to crossing the bridge and walking up the hill to Klein Schanze, the small park twenty minutes or so from home which, in those days, was one of the few open spaces in a city still largely defined by its defensible location upon the bend of the river Aare. From here, one could view the medieval city through the chimney smoke, and beyond – the snow-capped peaks of the Alps. Against this backdrop, the smallness of Bern, and even more the smallness of Albert Einstein, was both salutary and enervating. Albert was a mere speck beside the majesty of those mountains, yet he contained galaxies.

'Herr Doktor Einstein, it is good to see you looking so cheerful.' Startled, it took Albert a moment to recognise Freddy outside of his café.

'Herr Gründer.' He bowed. 'And Fraü Gründer, I presume. The progenitor of the most outstanding cake in Bern.'

The lady, who was fine-boned and, in her discreet yet fashionable plum dress, some distance from the matron Albert had always imagined elbow-deep in the mixing bowl, smiled in amusement.

'The Herr Doktor,' Freddy explained as they continued their promenade. 'Is one of my regular clients. He is a great mathematician.' Albert nodded. He was not about to correct him.

'You work at the Institute, Herr Doktor?'

'In the patents department, Fraù Gründer. I am required to examine mechanical inventions, check them for their originality, and if they *are* sufficiently original …'

'This is Switzerland,' interrupted Freddy. 'The land of inventions!'

'Quite,' said Albert. 'Then I draft a patent on behalf of the applicant.'

'Many fascinating ideas must have passed across your desk, Herr Doktor,' said Fraù Gründer. 'What was the most fantastic?'

'The most fantastic? Ah.' He scratched his head. Unlike the Gründers, he did not wear a hat outside – a fashion pertaining to intellectuals of the time. 'That would probably have to be the flying balloon.'

'Flying balloon?' said Fraù Gründer. 'But isn't that the point of balloons? To fly, I mean.'

'Precisely, Fraù Gründer, but this balloon had wings. Or rather, the design entailed a gentleman being strapped beneath it with mechanical wings operated with handles on either side, and a further one … ahem,' he glanced at Freddy who nodded for him to continue, 'strapped to his behind, rather like a rudder. For direction, you see.'

'It sounds like a splendid idea,' said Fraù Gründer. 'Did you grant it a patent?'

'I requested the applicant come back to me with proof that it worked. I have yet to hear from him.'

'What a shame! I would love to see something like that – imagine, we could be gazing across Bern now with the sky full of gentlemen and ladies attached to balloons.' She turned to her husband. 'You could have done with one of those yourself, my dear.'

Freddy puffed.

'My husband had a fall many years ago,' explained Fraù Gründer. 'But obviously, he survived. Hence the name of our café.'

'Of course!' exclaimed Albert. '*Lucky* Freddy's.' He was embarrassed that such was his self-absorption, he had never enquired about the origin of the establishment's name, which was particularly eccentric for a city like Bern where pubs and cafes were traditionally named after their location, such as 'Das Parkcafé' or 'Die Mittlestraße'.

'I used to be a master mason,' explained Freddy. He pointed to the spire of Bern Munster, rising above the smog. 'I was up there, right at the top, renovating the steeple, when I slipped. We had scaffolding, naturally, and I had a rope attached, but the scaffold gave way, and I went down.'

'From the very top?'

'The *very* top.' He made a slicing movement. 'Zip. One hundred and one metres.'

'That must have been terrifying, Freddy,' said Albert.

'It was …' he glanced at his wife. 'Surprising. Then annoying. I mean, I had plenty of time to think.'

Albert nodded. 'It might have seemed like that.'

'I was most annoyed with whoever had constructed the damn scaffolding!'

'And that you were going to leave a wife and three children, my dear,' interjected Fraù Gründer.

'Yes, that, of course, my dear. As I said, I had plenty of time to think while I plummeted. In fact, Herr Doktor, it barely felt like plummeting at all.'

'It wouldn't,' muttered Albert. 'You won't feel

your weight as you fall, only when you hit the ground.'

'Which, fortunately, I avoided because the plank attached to the rope caught on some guttering that started to detach, thereby causing my descent to slow and … Herr Doktor?' Albert was walking away. 'Herr Doktor!'

Albert raised his hand in salutation, and continued rapidly down the hill.

He arrived back in the apartment and, without even removing his coat, went straight to his desk. He reached for a fresh piece of paper and a pencil – he did not even have time to fiddle with his pen. For the rest of that afternoon, and on through the night, he wrote.

At some point, Albert must have drifted off because he found himself in a rocket leaving the earth. It was not dissimilar to the one he had seen with Mileva in the circus tent a few years earlier, possibly the first proper science fiction film – Georges Méliès' *Le voyage dans la lune* – whence an adventurer's rocket prongs a biscuit-shaped Moon featuring an ingeniously animated man's face, hitting him plumb in the eye (the first time Albert and Mileva had gasped, upon repeated visits it always made them laugh).

So Albert is in that tubular, sparking

contraption, leaning out to keep it on target, while at the same time astonished at his own good fortune to be among the stars when, what should appear beside his rocket, but another? He calls out (at the same time as knowing full well there is no sound in the vacuum of space) and who should peer through the porthole but Lieserl? And it is strange, because she is not the babe he knew, but the little girl he never did.

The rockets align and he leans out in an effort to open Lieserl's porthole, reach in and pluck her out but, just as his fingertips dab the glass, her rocket edges past. He watches helplessly as it overtakes his own and overshoots the Man in the Moon, who watches it glide by before looking back at him and raising an eyebrow.

Albert woke, drooling across his papers. The mantle clock was striking seven in the morning. He stood up, still in his overcoat, and went to the bathroom. He splashed some water on his face and had a pee. Before he went back out, he stopped beside the desk and stared down at his equations. He shuffled through the pages scattered in front of him and found the first. He plucked his pen from its well and scribbled along the top: *A Geometric Theory of Gravitation.*

'Herr Doktor, are you all right? We were worried about you.'

'Hm? Yes, thank you, Freddy.' Albert looked at him expectantly, he was in no mood for chitchat. Freddy got the message.

'*Kafi-crème* and a slice of *Rüeblitorte*, coming up, Herr Doktor.'

'Actually, make that two slices, please, Freddy.'

'Certainly, Herr Doktor.'

That evening Albert left work early to catch the post office but, when he arrived at the queue for the telegram, he realised he was short of cash and would have to keep his word count to a minimum.

He scratched his head.

'It's to Mileva Marić,' he told the clerk. 'Return home. STOP. I need you. STOP. New theory. STOP. Relativity. STOP.'

Notes

1. Albert Einstein recounted how as a young man in Bern in 1907 a thought had 'startled' him: 'If a person falls freely, he will not feel his own weight.' He called this 'the happiest thought in my life.'

2. Einstein married Elsa Löwenthal in 1919, having begun an affair with her in 1912, two years before Mileva left him for good.

3. One of the conditions of Mileva's divorce settlement was that if Albert were to ever win the Nobel Prize, she would receive the prize money. When he was finally granted the award in 1921, he handed the entire sum - a dozen times his annual salary as a university professor - to Mileva. She lived off the interest for the rest of her life.

———

Tom Benjamin grew up in the suburbs of north London and began his working life as a journalist before becoming a spokesman for Scotland Yard. He later moved into public health, where he developed Britain's first national campaign against alcohol abuse, Know Your Limits, and led drugs awareness programme FRANK. He now lives in Bologna. Tom's critically-acclaimed, Bologna-set Daniel Leicester series has been optioned for TV by Free@LastTV. Find Tom via the links below:

https://www.amazon.co.uk/dp/B09D2XTT99

Twitter/X: @Tombenjaminsays

Instagram: @Tombenjaminsays

Facebook: @Tombenjaminsays

WELL PLAYED, SON

ANNA JEFFERSON

I t's not like I didn't have other interests. I did. Do: football. American football on Sky. Tennis. But yeah, mainly rugby. That had nothing to do with Dad. I would have been interested in it even if he wasn't. It's completely got nothing to do with him. Yes, it's good that he liked to watch it. And there are all his trophies in the cabinet in the games room. And those of Grandad Robert as well. The photographs of the old rugby players are mental. These skinny men with floppy hair. There's a picture of Grandad Robert eating an orange segment and smoking a fag at half time. He still scored the winning try in that game. Dad made it to the Counties as well. He used to go and practice every Thursday and play every Sunday. Rugby widow, mum used to call herself, but I know she was pleased when I started playing.

See, I'm not clever like Paul, I've never been good at anything at school apart from sport. So, this was *my* thing. I don't mean to sound like I'm ten, but couldn't he have chosen something different, like being a brain surgeon or an engineer? He can write as well, so he could have done that. Or if he did want to do sport, he could have chosen a different one. It didn't need to be rugby too, did it? Yes, I realise it was easier for Dad to drop us both off for practice and yes, I get it that him and Uncle

Keith used to both play, and that a bit of healthy rivalry is OK, but still.

He's a school year younger than me, that counts for something. These were my mates, my crew. I didn't mean half the shit I said to him in front of the team, but he's got to know his place, right? He had to understand that this was my team, I was Vice Captain. That meant something. And he hadn't really been playing that long, and so last in was always going to get a bit of shit from the team. It's just banter. It's just a bit of fun.

The home match against Lincoln was a big deal. A huge deal. Everyone wants to get noticed by a scout, it's the dream, right? Plucked from obscurity (that's the right word, isn't it? Pretty sure Paul would tell me it's not) and go from zero to hero. One minute you're fucking up your GCSEs and then next, boom, fast track to the good life with no looking back. I wasn't interested in the fame, although I would sometimes dream about what it would be like to be Jonny Wilkinson. Boys want to be you; girls want to be with you. But really, I just wanted to be good at something. Anything, really.

I remember the first time Dad came to watch me play. Standing on the sidelines, his breath coming out in little puffs of cold cloud, he was blowing on his hands and stamping his feet. There was frost on the ground, it was fucking brutal. It was a good match. I scored a try against Scunthorpe. And afterwards, as we walked towards the car, he smiled and nodded at me, then said, 'well played, son.'

See, Paul is Mum's favourite. But I was no one's favourite until that point. Then Dad started showing an interest in me. He got out the old home videos of his games when he was not much older than me, he knew each one by heart and would talk me through the game, move by move. What went well; what he wished he'd done differently. It was pretty boring on the whole, and the recordings were really grainy, so it wasn't even that easy to make Dad out, but I'd never really watched anything with Dad before, so there was that.

Paul would come in and watch it as well and ask questions and I was just like, fuck the fuck off. Go sit with Mum in the kitchen and she can tell you how the sun shines out your arse. But Dad would answer his questions, and I'd be sitting there like a warm shit in a salad waiting for him to leave. I'd give him the eye, but he'd pretend he hadn't seen and then, this one time, Dad asked him if he was interested in playing rugby and I'm thinking, course he's not. He's never shown any interest. None. So I didn't even bother giving him the eye that time as I knew the answer would be no, but would you and Adam and fucking Eve it, he said, and I kid you not, yeah, I'll give it a go.

Yeah. I'll give it a go.

He could do anything. Anything. Be a maths genius or a scuba diver. He could get into climbing, or running, he's good at fucking running away from shit so why didn't he go and do that?

Instead, he joined the school team and Dad started taking us both to practice. He was shit, but not the worst. There are worse players on the field, but I'd never tell him that. So Dad was then cheering for the two of us.

I just don't know why he didn't say no to Dad. He wouldn't have cared. I was playing. And he said, 'well played, son,' to me. I've never heard him say that to Paul. Cos he's never played well.

But then there was the match against Lincoln and the talent scout was meant to come. It was just a rumour. You never know if they do or not, cos that's their thing. They turn up when you least expect it, like a security guard in Curry's when you've got a games console down your kecks and they creep up behind you and say, 'young man, I don't think you've paid for that.'

But Coach had heard that there was a guy up from Leicester who was doing the rounds of the school games. Looking out for raw talent, that's what he called it. Raw talent, whatever the fuck that meant. And that he was 99% sure he was going to be at the match.

Everyone was talking about it in the changing room, but it was like a joke. As if Megan Fox was going to be watching and would be asking someone out afterwards. They were all giddy but no one expected to get picked. And it wasn't guaranteed that he was even coming, other than Coach saying it was 99% certain.

As we ran out onto the pitch, I looked around at who was watching. Mainly dads and girlfriends. And only girlfriends who'd been around for a while. You wouldn't get up that early on a Sunday morning to watch someone who might dump you the next week. Stay in bed and watch Ramsay's Kitchen Nightmares instead, I'd say. I looked around and then saw him. He stood out like a pork chop at a bat mitzvah, in his leather jacket and woolly hat. Everyone knew. And I could feel the blood pumping through my veins, my muscles twitching. I looked at Dad and he nodded; he knew too. And I deserved it. Well played, son.

The first half of the game was good, but not brilliant. Lincoln were dirty. They played like animals. I kept my focus. Even when Paul missed a throw, I didn't shout at him, didn't call him a prick. I just reset and continued. Professional.

I bossed it after half-time. My muscles ached, but I gave no shits. Tearing up that pitch like it was nothing. Two tries. I was on fire. Lincoln hated me. But I saw the scout write something in his little notebook, licking the end of the pencil before writing like a fucking pervert. Then he looked up and at me. Directly in the eye. That's when I knew I'd got it. But don't be cocky, Luke, I told myself. We still have two minutes left to play. I'm not Will Carling yet. There's no glory until the whistle is blown. Everyone knows that.

And then it happened.

It was my ball. I'd called it. But someone had shouted Paul. He thought it was his. Prick. So, he ran for it, looking up not out. Didn't see me, he said. But I'm a big fucking guy. You don't not see me. But he looked up not out and smashed straight into me. Catching my ball but knocking me clean over. That's rugby. That's the game. But I landed on my elbow. I knew before the pain even started to shoot along my arm, through my body, that it was shattered. That the angle it was pointing at was all wrong.

Paul just looked at me. Mouth open like a demented fish. Face white as if all the blood had drained from it, as if it was him whose olecranon and ulna had crushed together like smashing wet sand against a wall. Yeah, I had no idea what they were called before either but, after hours of surgery and physio, you get to know all the shit you never needed to know before.

So. Game over. They say I might be able to play again in time. But what for? Why would I want to stand around like a pussy playing for the B team. Sitting on the subs bench. Poor Luke. Remember when he was good? Put him in reserve. Give him a run out for a bit. No thanks. I'd prefer just to get fucked up. All the fun without the early morning training sessions. It's not like I was ever going to pass my A levels anyway. They let me repeat a year. That was cos of Dad. He gives a lot to the school, not time or shit like that. Money. He paid for the football pitch to be AstroTurfed. And for a new industrial cooker when their one blew up. So yeah, they owed him. But they won't do it again. I know that.

Fucking ridiculous that I'm in the same school year as Paul now. Him and all his dickhead mates. The lasses like me though. Course they do. They like a bit of mental. A bit of unpredictable. Luke Riley? Yeah, he's nuts.

And Paul. Fucking Paul. He's applied to study

Sports Science at uni. Not Astrophysics or fucking politics or whatever. Sports Science. Like he just wanted to shit directly in my face.

Dad doesn't ask me to watch the rugby any more. He doesn't ask anyone, so that's something at least. He put his videos back up in the loft. He said I can come and work for him when I finish school. A pity job. Thanks a fucking lot. I'll probably do it, cos what else am I going to do? But they'll all know. All those pricks who work for him. They'll all know I'm the boss's son and I can't even get my own job. But I could have done. I could be training with the best now. Fuck it. That's life, eh? That's life, as they say. Might as well go get fucked up in the pub now. So, yeah. There's always that.

ANNA JEFFERSON IS a fiction writer and playwright, having written for stage and screen since 2005, and is represented by Curtis Brown. She has published three novels, *Winging It* (2020) and *Nailing It* (2021), both published with Orion, and *Happiness Lives Next Door*, published with Penguin Random House, Germany (2024.) She is currently writing her fourth novel. Her first short film script, *Rudy Can't Fail,* was produced by Makelight Productions in 2014 and screened at BFI Flare, GAZE Festival, Dublin, MIX Copenhagen and London Short Film Festival. Anna is founder and co-director of Broken Leg Theatre and has written and toured five plays nationally. She is Artistic Director at New Writing South, the literature development agency for the South East. Anna lives in Brighton with her husband and two children. Find Anna and her books via the links below.

https://annajefferson.co.uk/

https://www.amazon.co.uk/stores/Anna-Jefferson/author/B07RFQCHN9

Twitter/X: @annajefferson

Instagram: @annasianjeffersonauthor

THE LOCKET

PAULA GREENLEES

October leaves sparkled and crackled on the bonfire. I swept another pile from the garden path onto the flames, my scar tingling in the heat. I ran my hand over my skin and felt the ridged line across my face. Behind me, the melody of the children's swings accompanied the rhythmic sweeping of my broom. Side by side, Beatrice and Amy flew higher, their laughter rising with the motion of their game.

'Mummy, look, we can touch the sky!' Beatrice shouted, her ladybird wellingtons in danger of falling from her feet.

'Don't go too high,' I warned, walking towards them. 'Amy's only little. You need to look after her.'

'OK, Mummy. I'll look after her.' Beatrice giggled and Amy shrieked but neither of them slowed down.

I returned to my chore, sweeping defiant leaves that danced in the gentle wind. Beyond the flames, I heard the garden gate click, the purr of an engine idling and footsteps on the gravel path.

'Who is it?' I shouted. My eyes watered as I peered through the smoke towards the gate. I listened as footsteps came towards me, then a figure appeared – just visible through the smoke.

'Registered, love. Needs signing for.'

I put the broom down and signed the form,

then took the packet from the postman's outstretched hand. Immediately, I knew who had sent it – I guessed before I saw the writing.

Louisa.

Since we met again at our mother's funeral a year ago, her letters had arrived at regular intervals. I'd only read the first one, full of remorse and begging for reconciliation. However, I could tell it wasn't just a letter this time. As the postman's footsteps retreated, I fingered the envelope and I felt a lump, as though there was something small inside. I turned it over in my hands, then I stepped forward, ready to thrust it into the fire.

'Mummy's got a letter, letter, letter! Mummy's got a letter!' The girls chanted from the swings that were now slowing down. 'Who's it from, Mummy?' Amy squinted, her tiny hand over her eyes.

Beatrice looked at me, her face bright with expectation, 'Aren't you going to open it?'

I looked at their eager faces. I hesitated but then tore the packet open. Something gold and shiny fell into my hand. I held it for a second before it slipped onto the ground between my feet. It was my mother's locket. As it fell from my hand, the memories came flooding back …

.   .   .

'HAS ANYONE SEEN MY LOCKET? I took it off before my bath. I'm sure I put it on my dressing table.'

Our mother, tall and majestic, stood framed by the kitchen doorway. She wore a white silk dressing gown, and her hair was freshly washed and dried in a crisp bob. Her face was still glowing and pink from the heat of the bath. Hints of perfume and hairspray wafted towards me.

Louisa, nineteen and two years my senior, and I sat in silence as far away from each other as possible at the kitchen table. We both sipped glasses of Pimm's and sat upright on hearing her voice. We continued to slice fruit and cucumber into elegant portions for expectant jugs, taking care to avoid spoiling our smart new party dresses. Louisa held the paring knife in her hand.

'No, Mum, I haven't.' She jabbed the knife towards me without lifting her face. 'Try asking *her*.'

'I haven't seen it, either,' I said, examining a strawberry in my hand.

'Oh, come on you two, surely you've made up now?' Mum crossed her arms.

Louisa said nothing but continued to chop cucumber in stiff, heavy strokes.

'Oh, for goodness' sake you two!' My mother tightened the belt on her dressing gown. 'Why can't you ever get on? It's been like this all holiday.' She looked from Louisa to me then back again. 'Well, just try tonight, please. Try putting someone else first for a change.'

I mumbled, 'Sorry,' as I kept my eyes on the fruit I was chopping. 'I'll try, OK.'

'I'll keep an eye out for it, Mum.' I heard a sudden brightness in Louisa's voice. 'The locket is bound to turn up.'

'Well, I hope so. Everyone will be here in half an hour and I'm running desperately behind. I must get dressed.' She left the room; her perfume lingered for a moment, then it faded along with her authority.

We continued to work in uncomfortable silence, aware of each other, yet avoiding conversation. That was until I noticed Louisa smirking; it was a smile full of self-satisfaction. It made my jaw tense, and I felt an angry pounding in my head.

'What are you looking so smug about?' I asked, throwing mint into a jug.

Louisa turned her head towards me. 'You'll find out soon enough.'

'What's that supposed to mean?'

She said nothing but continued to grin like the Cheshire cat.

'You're up to something.' I bit into a strawberry and felt the juice dribble down my chin. I wiped the juice away, covering my fingers in sticky liquid. I licked them before the juice ran onto my pale lemon dress. 'I know that look.'

Louisa began to laugh. 'You think you're so clever, don't you, Elsa?' She pointed a long, freshly painted red nail at me. 'You think you know everything, but you don't.'

I tore a sprig of mint apart and stared at her heavily made-up face. Despite the mask, I detected something that gave her away. 'It was you, wasn't it?'

'What was?'

'You've hidden the locket.'

'No, I haven't.' She stopped chopping, the knife glinted in her hand. She stared directly at me.

'Yes, you have. You took the locket when you went to the loo. I bet you've hidden it in my room.'

She stood up, and her chair flew behind her. 'You deserve to get punished, you little bitch!'

'Why, because you got into trouble about last night? At least I didn't tell them where you were; you'd be grounded for a month if they knew.'

'You're just jealous, because you're an ugly runt and haven't got a boyfriend yourself.' Her eyes narrowed and she came towards me. 'You're an ugly little runt and I hate you. I always have.'

'Why? Why do you hate me so much?' I asked. I

backed away from her until I reached the wall. 'You've always been horrid to me, always!'

'Where do I start? All my favourite toys you broke, mother taking your side as you were younger. Then, how many times have you told tales on me, blaming me for breaking mother's figurines, cracking her favourite mirror, ruining her silk dress with black ink and pointing the finger at me. I wish you'd never been born.'

'Well, I don't like you that much either.'

'Really?' she jeered. 'Bet you couldn't hate me as much as I hate you. You spoil everything.'

Tears welled in my eyes. I struggled to stop them falling. Louisa thrust her face into mine, 'I wish you were gone, Elsa, I wish you were dead. I wish it more than anything I've ever wished for in my life.'

She spat in my face. The tears began to fall, but no sound came. I felt the pressure that had been building in my head explode out of my skull, and my hand contacted the soft flesh on her cheek.

'You fucking little cow!' she shouted and grabbed my hair. The roots burnt as she pulled them. It was agony. I kicked her in the shins and pushed her hard. She fell back against the table, splashing a jug of Pimm's, the contents sloshing onto the table. I ran towards the door.

'I'm going to tell Mum,' I yelled.

'Do you think she'll believe you?' Louisa's lips contorted with contempt. 'You're just a little liar! You've always wanted that locket. She'll think you've made it up to get me into even more trouble. You're always telling tales, Elsa, how can anyone believe a word you say?'

'But I didn't steal the locket.' My hand touched the doorknob. 'She'll believe me this time.'

Louisa strode towards me. There was a look in her eyes that frightened me. I pushed her away, hitting her in the chest. Her features hardened. In one sudden, swift movement her hand flew up to my face, metal gleaming as her arm arced. I screamed. Louisa froze. I put my hand to my face.

I felt something warm and moist coat my fingers. I lowered them and examined them, not quite comprehending what I saw. Something darker than strawberry juice covered my hand. I looked towards Louisa. Her arm hung by her side, the paring knife in her hand. The colour drained from her face, and she dropped the knife onto the floor. My legs began to shake. I looked down at the folds of my lemon skirt and watched crimson stains swelling like ink on the silk. My knees buckled beneath me, and the room swirled into a white mist against the background of Louisa's panicked cries.

. . .

A SHRIEK INTERRUPTED MY THOUGHTS. Beatrice and Amy stood in front of me. Beatrice held a clump of Amy's hair in her hand. Amy's face was scarlet as she kicked and screamed at her sister.

'What on earth is going on?' I demanded.

'I told her to give it back, Mummy,' Beatrice explained, pointing to Amy's hand, 'but she wouldn't listen.'

'Mummy dropped it,' Amy began. Tears dangled from her thick, dark eyelashes. She swallowed and then gasped for air as though it was her final breath. 'Amy wants it.'

I looked down at her hand, clasped tightly in her fist was the locket. The chain dangled, giving away her secret. She followed my line of sight and added, 'S' pretty.'

I bent down to Amy's level. 'It's Mummy's, Amy. Please, can I have it back?'

I reached out and took the locket from her hand. It was open and inside were photographs of Louisa and me as young children, holding hands and smiling. Beatrice stood at my side and peered intently at the photographs.

'Who are the little girls in the pictures?' she asked. 'Are they us?'

'No, they're not, but they look a bit like you.' I shut the locket. 'They're little girls who were sisters a long time ago.'

'Why aren't they sisters now?' Beatrice asked. 'Did they go to Heaven?'

'No, they, well, they just got separated from each other.'

Beatrice bit her lip. She moved towards Amy and placed her arm around her shoulder. 'I'm never going to lose Amy.'

'No, you mustn't, Beatrice. You must never lose Amy. You must always look after each other.' I smiled at her. 'But now you should say sorry to Amy for pulling her hair. You know it's wrong. How would you like it if someone did that to you?'

Beatrice planted a kiss on Amy's tear-stained cheek. 'Sorry I hurt you. I'll look after you forever and ever, no matter what.'

'And Amy, you should say sorry, too. It takes two to make an argument, and two to make up.'

Amy hugged Beatrice and kissed her back. 'Love you, too.' She looked back at me with large, innocent eyes, searching for approval.

A film of mist clouded my vision, and a tear escaped; the truth of what I had just said dawned on me.

'Don't cry, Mummy,' Beatrice touched my arm, 'I didn't want to hurt Amy. She's my bestest friend.'

I pulled the girls towards me and held them to my chest. 'Mummy's not cross with you. You haven't made me cry.' Their arms wrapped around each other, and I stroked Beatrice's soft, wispy hair.

'Can't breathe, Mummy,' Amy muttered. 'You're squashing me.' I released them both, stood up and stroked their faces with my hand. I wiped away the stubborn tears falling from my eyes with my thumb.

'O-oh!' Beatrice pointed towards Louisa's letter, which I'd dropped. It blew towards the fire, encouraged by a hearty gust of wind. I ran towards it and tried in vain to catch it. The fire drew it in, and flames engulfed the paper. I picked up a stick from the ground and tried to snatch it out; too late, the edges of the envelope blackened and curled. I stood staring at the blue flames, which erupted into large orange flares.

'Naughty wind!' Amy came and stood next to me. 'Naughty, naughty fire!'

'I didn't have a chance to read it,' I said, staring into the fire. 'I didn't find out what she had to say, why she decided after all this time to send me the locket.'

Beatrice joined us and held my hand. 'Never

mind, Mummy.' She squeezed. 'You can still write to say thank you for your present.'

I squeezed her hand back, a little too tight. After all this time, watching my daughters, hoping that they would always be friends and never fall out, my argument with Louisa at last seemed futile. Was it too late to turn back the clock? Yes, but while there was a future there was hope, and it had taken the innocence of a child to make me see it.

'Yes, Beatrice,' I said, gazing at her hopeful face. 'You're right. Perhaps I should.'

PAULA GREENLEES HAS LIVED in various places, including Singapore, where she was based for three years. It was while living in Singapore that the first seeds of her debut novel, *Journey to Paradise* developed. Her writing, although set against exotic backgrounds, is set on the cusp of change. She likes to dig into a variety of issues, and her main protagonist is, in many ways, a metaphor for the events surrounding her at that time. Paula has a degree in English and European Thought and Literature, and a Master's Degree in Creative Writing. When she's not writing, you can find her people-watching in cafés, exploring the countryside by foot or travelling to faraway places. She is a keen amateur photographer. Follow Paula via the links below to see what she is up to!

www.paulagreenlees.com

Twitter/X: @PGreenlees

Instagram: @paulagreenlees

Facebook: @writingmatter

CONNECTION

SARAH MOORHEAD

I t was the biggest turd, dog or otherwise, that he had ever seen. It lay steaming on the rain-washed London pavement, glistening in the rays of the re-emerging sun. Romy poked at it with a piece of wire that he'd rescued from a nearby skip. Suddenly, he was jerked upwards by the hood of his anorak, the collar almost crushing his seven-year-old throat.

'What ya doin'? Dirty bugger!' screeched his Aunt Cecilly. Some of his immature dreads had been included in that handful. Romy rubbed his head.

'Ya wanna catch sum'tin? Ya wanna get sick?'

At eye level to her vast belly, he watched the button straining to keep the two sides of her raincoat together.

'Grab m' bag, Jerome. Don't let go.'

Cecilly bustled him into the Elephant and Castle tube station and, as she chose her route, Romy stared up at the rainbow of the underground map. He traced the line from the station as though it was a 'Can you guess which string leads to the balloon?' game in his puzzle book. He liked the name of their line, but not the colour.

'Bakerloo, Bakerloo,' he repeated to himself rhythmically. He particularly liked the bit between

Paddington and Edgware Road, as it reminded him of the flag on his big brother's wall.

'It looks like spaghetti,' he said. Spaghetti that had been coloured in with felt-tip pens.

Guided by his Aunt Cecilly, Romy squashed into the huge lift, trapped amid a forest of tree-legs in brown cotton, blue denim and floral skirts, the musty smell of the station combining with his aunt's overwhelming lavender perfume.

'Auntie, how would an elephant get up the stairs?'

'What ya talkin' about?'

'Them spiral staircases in castles. If an elephant lived there, they couldn't go upstairs to bed. They'd be too big. Big feet, little steps.'

'What do ya know about spirals?'

'Mrs Tomlin taught us.'

'Hush now, child. Ev'body in dis lift tink ya an idiot, boy.'

Down, down into the soil they went, through the layers of rock, deep underground, maybe even to the earth's core. The lift juddered to a halt and a brief hiatus ensued during which Romy imagined what was on the other side of the grey metal concertinaed door. It rattled and screeched open and instead of red-hot magma, he saw a curved pale-beige tunnel.

A low rumble rose from the bowels of the underground. It moved closer, vibrating through his body before coming to a halt. Romy bounced off Cecilly's ample hips as they made their way along the corridor. Massive posters, much bigger than him, sprawled the walls, the bright hues contrasting with the dull colour of the tiles that reminded Romy of the swimming baths. Open-mouthed, he stared at the singers and dancers who seemed to be leaping out at him, until the view was obscured by a sudden surge of people pouring into the narrow space. He felt carried along on the wave of travellers, until he was disorientated and his feet no longer seemed to touch the floor and his fingers slipped away from his aunt's bag.

Suddenly the tunnel emptied as people filtered into the tube train or up the steps to the exit. The sudden emptiness and silence made him feel as though he was underwater.

Romy stood still on the vacated platform. Where was his aunt? Which direction had he come from? How was he going to get home?

He suddenly realised that he was not on his own. A figure stood nearby, one that made him think that a character from the posters had come to life. Ancient and bedraggled, the vagabond lurched forward and grabbed Romy roughly by the wrist.

Panic-stricken, the boy tried to wriggle free from the vice-like grip of the stranger.

The man had bright, wild eyes hidden in a mass of matted hair. His clothes were ripped and stained, his breath reeked. He reached into the pocket of his overcoat.

Romy tried to shout for his aunt, but all that came out was, 'Aaaah!'

The man produced a small piece of once-white card, creased and bent at the corners. He held it up. 'You like the underground,' he said, his voice sounding as though he had not spoken for a long time. 'Like me,' he hissed and grinned, his teeth grey-brown like tombstones. He pressed the card into the boy's hand and then let go.

Romy, intrigued, no longer felt the impulse to run away. His hand momentarily remained mid-air where the man had left it, holding a mini-map of the tube system.

'For you,' said the man and Romy broke into a huge smile. He brought the card close to his face and located Edgware Road.

'Come on,' said the vagrant, stalking off towards a vending machine. The boy looked both ways hesitatingly before trotting after him.

'You like chocolate?' he asked Romy, who did not look up, but nodded.

What would Cecilly say, accepting sweets from a stranger? *Don't eat dat stuff, it rat your teeth.* She always pronounced 'rot' as 'rat'. Romy eyed the tracks wondering if there were any rats on the line. The man held out a fist, nails black and ragged, fingers yellow with nicotine, which opened out like a flower to reveal a palmful of brown five pence pieces. The desire for chocolate overcame the repulsion at the dirt and Romy took the coins and put them into the slot.

The two of them sat together on the grey plastic seats, sharing the sweet silently.

Finally Romy found his voice. 'Do you live here?'

'Yes.'

'You don't see the sun?' the boy asked, incredulous.

'Not for a long time.'

There was a pause.

'Do you brush your hair?' he asked the man.

'Do you brush yours?' came the reply.

Romy smiled, put another piece of chocolate into his mouth, and sighed.

A few moments later, the man stood up and disappeared through the gap towards the opposite platform. Seconds later, he appeared again.

'Get up, son!' He beckoned the boy forward.

'Come on!' Seeing the wild, excited look in the man's eyes again Romy became apprehensive but, intrigued, he followed. He heard a distant rumble.

The man's decrepit shoes danced on the yellow line that his aunt had warned Romy about. He could feel panic rising in his stomach, which grew as the tramp closed his eyes and began to sway gently and hum to himself. The track reverberated with the oncoming tube train.

Romy's heartbeat increased as the vibrations became stronger and the man's humming became louder, as if he was joining in with the train's song.

'Sometimes,' whispered the man, lurching backwards and forwards now, 'I'm scared that I might jump!' His eyes flicked open and settled on the boy. 'Ready … ready …'

Romy felt himself swaying in time with the man, mesmerised. He started to feel dizzy. What if he fainted and fell onto the track? What if he couldn't climb up onto the platform in time?

'Here it comes! Here it comes!' the man was chanting, a deep growling rising from the gaping blackness of the tunnel mouth.

It's a monster! thought Romy. Then a strange desire welled up in him, as if his body wanted to leap right onto the track, but his mind was shouting *No! No! Don't do it!*

The growling turned into a loud roar and the man shouted, 'Here we go!'

Romy held his breath and, suddenly, there was the most delicious rush of warm air curling all around him, comforting and soothing, like Jamaican waves. As it died down there was an ear-splitting *whoosh* as the tube train blasted into the station, terrifying and exhilarating at the same time.

The doors gushed open and the next thing that he knew his aunt was shouting at him and pulling him towards her.

'Jerome! Jerome! Oh, my boy!' Cecilly grabbed him and hugged him so hard that he could not turn his head towards his new friend.

She dragged him back towards the opposite platform where their train had already pulled in. As the doors shut behind them, Cecilly let go.

The train began to pull away. Romy rested his forehead on the glass, locking eyes with the man left standing on the platform, until he could no longer see, still clutching his map as a reminder of their connection.

―――――――

BORN IN LIVERPOOL, **Sarah Moorhead** has told stories since childhood and uses writing as bubblegum for her over-active brain – to keep it out of trouble. Fascinated by meaning, motivation and mystery, she studied Theology at university. Over the last twenty-nine years, apart from teaching in a secondary school, Sarah has attained a black belt in kickboxing, worked as a chaplain, established a Justice and Peace youth group, and written articles for newspapers and magazines about her work in education and religion. She has written true crime podcast scripts for Noiser/Spotify and now interviews other authors in Waterstones. She is a coach at the Bestseller Writing Academy. She still lives in her beloved hometown with her husband, two sons and her beloved Black Lab, Seamus. You can find out more about Sarah here: https://sarahmoorhead.com and via her Amazon Author Page here: https://www.amazon.co.uk/stores/Sarah-Moorhead/author/B0C2L66GS1

A LITTLE, LOST

TIM EWINS

Idris couldn't tell you what he had for breakfast that day and he couldn't tell you what he wore to work. He couldn't even tell you if he went to work at all. The day was completely insignificant to Idris, until about 3.30 p.m. that is.

Idris remembered every tiny thing after 3.30 p.m. in detail. He didn't want to, but he did, often. He'd been sitting in a dark room on a blue plastic chair holding his wife Amy's hand. Idris remembered every movement he'd seen on Amy's face, every word the nurse had said and where every one of Amy's tears had fallen on her cheek before being wiped off onto her sleeve.

At 3.28 p.m. the nurse had rubbed gel on Amy's stomach. You couldn't see any difference in Amy's size, but she'd told Idris she was certain she could feel the baby with her hand when she tried. A second nurse brought down a widescreen TV on a flexible stand on the wall. Idris squeezed Amy's hand and they both watched the screen.

'There it is,' Amy said softly and Idris smiled without moving his eyes from the screen. He could see it too. A clear outline of their baby. Head, body and limbs. Then the nurse said the words that Idris remembered better than anything else that day.

'Amy, I'm so sorry, sweetheart.' Idris looked at the nurse. 'There's no heartbeat.'

9 WEEKS BEFORE

He sat on the bed and waited for Amy to come out of the bathroom. They'd been having sex every other day for the past two months. Not being a couple to cancel old traditions, they'd had sex every Saturday too. Today was Saturday. Idris picked up his Kindle and started to read. He'd wait for Amy to come back to bed, have sex, feed the dog and make coffee for Amy and himself. Saturday mornings were pretty good.

The bedroom door opened, and he looked up and smiled. Amy looked tense and there was a couple of seconds' silence whilst they looked at each other.

'I'm a little bit pregnant,' Amy said and Idris jumped to the side of the bed.

'Are you kidding?' He looked at the stick. 'Boom!'

'Yep.' They hugged, and Idris felt the top of Amy's head on the bottom of his chin.

Amy was adamant that they couldn't tell anyone

yet and, as the baby would take nine months to actually come, there wasn't really anything to do now. They couldn't even celebrate with a glass of wine.

'Go and wake up the dog,' she suggested, 'we can tell him at least.'

'Um … it's Saturday,' Idris pointed out, jokingly gyrating his hips on the bed. Amy smiled at him and played with her hair seductively whilst biting her lip.

'Nope,' she said letting go of her hair, 'go get the dog.'

7 WEEKS BEFORE

It was raining outside, and the lounge was that nice kind of dark that only seems to happen late on a Sunday. Idris and Amy hadn't done much – Idris had cooked, Amy had played tug of war with the dog and they'd both watched a bad film on Channel Five.

'How shall we tell the family? Amy asked. Idris thought for a second.

'A lot of people make videos which end on the mum's tummy' he suggested, but Amy pulled a yuk face. Idris liked making videos but Amy had already claimed to be feeling sorry for the baby.

'You're going to film the poor thing all the time, let it have the next eight months to grow,' she said. Idris continued to think.

'What about a stop-motion of the whole pregnancy. You could dress in your dinosaur onesie as your tummy gets bigger and at the end, we could get the baby a dinosaur onesie too.' Amy pulled a more exaggerated yuk face, this time with her tongue out.

'I think we want people to know about the baby before it's born' she said sarcastically, and Idris pulled her a duh face.

'At the end of the video, you could pretend to eat the baby,' Idris suggested before getting a soft punch in the arm from his wife. The dog's tail wagged.

'Let's just invite people over after the first scan,' Amy said, 'but you can do your stop-motion if you want.'

'Four couples fight to win £1,000 in a new Couples Come Dine With Me,' came the voice-over from the TV. Idris put his arm around Amy, and she fell asleep.

3.50 P.M. THAT DAY

Amy usually put her head in her hands when she cried or she'd look away, but now she wasn't trying to hide. Idris was doing all he could to hold his tears back, for her, but he too was failing. He was silent for Amy's sake, but she'd be able to see how wet his cheeks were. Why had the nurse shown them the screen? The screen had made it real. That was the only time they'd ever see their baby.

A different nurse came into the room.

'I'm so sorry,' she said, tilting her head, 'if you want, I can send the photos of the scan to your address. Some people want that, it's up to you.' Idris shook his head to say no, and Amy murmured a barely audible agreement.

'OK,' the nurse said quietly.

'Do we get our £20 back?' Idris asked in a cracked voice, trying to make Amy smile. It worked, a bit.

'Of course,' the nurse answered seriously, 'aw, bless you. I am sorry.' Then she tilted her head again.

1 WEEK BEFORE

Idris and Amy had specifically wanted three bedrooms last year when they'd been looking to buy their first house. At the very least, they wanted a large spare room. What they ended up with was a small spare room. But Kirsty and Phil had taught them well, and so they'd compromised.

Idris had set up a camera for the dinosaur baby time-lapse in the small room. He'd wanted the room to change into a nursery at the same time as Amy's dinosaur onesie bump grew bigger in the video. Amy had bought a big picture of a hot air balloon for the baby which they'd hung together. Now they were struggling to make a cupboard with newly purchased wood. After leaning the newly cut wardrobe door against the wall to check its size, Idris stepped backwards and knocked the camera. He swore.

'That'll ruin the time-lapse,' he complained. Amy touched his shoulders.

'It doesn't matter,' she said.

That night, at 2.47 a.m., Amy sat up in bed. 'I've got a bad feeling,' she told Idris, who was only semi-awake. 'Something doesn't feel right.' At 3.01 they were both asleep again.

1 DAY BEFORE

Idris turned off the TV, put the dog to bed and woke up Amy, who had fallen asleep on the sofa. They'd enjoyed a night like any other.

'Come on,' he said, and Amy smiled with her eyes still closed, 'let's go to bed.' They'd both forgotten Amy's night-time panic by the time they'd woken up the morning after.

'Scan tomorrow,' Amy said sleepily, 'we're going to see our baby.'

4.15 P.M. THAT DAY

Both Idris and Amy were silent during the car journey home. Idris drove with one hand on the steering wheel and one hand on Amy's leg.

How he wished there had been a heartbeat. They should be going home to tell their friends and family the good news but instead … well, he didn't know. Should they tell people? Maybe they should keep it a secret and pretend to be fine. All of a sudden, he couldn't work out why they'd kept the pregnancy a secret until the twelve week scan. Had it been for them or for the benefit of other people? He looked at Amy. If it wasn't for her, he'd be alone, and if it wasn't for him, so would she.

2 WEEKS AFTER

Idris and Amy sat in front of the TV together. Idris wasn't paying any attention to the screen, but he was grateful for the sound. The operation was booked for tomorrow.

Amy had been carrying the baby for two weeks now, knowing that it would never be born. Idris had been working from home in case she needed to go to the hospital before the operation. They'd been told that the miscarriage had happened at twelve weeks and that if the baby came before the operation it would look like a small foetus and it would hurt.

And so, Idris and Amy sat in front of the TV together but neither paid attention to the screen. Amy was looking at her phone, researching miscarriages, trying to regain some control. She wasn't used to not feeling in control. Idris knew his wife felt weak; when he looked at her, all he saw was strength.

8 WEEKS AFTER

'I wish I'd kept the photo,' Amy said as they lay in bed together. They'd had sex but not for the purposes of getting pregnant. Idris looked up from his Kindle. 'The scan,' she said. They hadn't talked much about the miscarriage since it had happened, although Idris knew that they'd both thought about it often.

'Why?' Idris asked.

'Because,' Amy said, 'it's gone.'

1 YEAR AFTER

Idris and Amy went to work, they walked the dog, they watched crap TV, they cooked, and they ate. Everything was the same except that it wasn't. Not quite. Two of their friends had fallen pregnant without telling them, the small spare room had become storage and Idris felt empty. Something that had never really been in their lives was missing.

Today was Saturday. Idris sat on the bed and waited for Amy to come out of the bathroom; she was doing an ovulation test. He'd wait for Amy to come back to bed, have sex, wake up the dog, feed the dog and make coffee for Amy and himself. Saturday mornings were still pretty good.

The bedroom door opened, and Idris looked up and smiled. Amy looked tense and there was a couple of seconds' silence as Idris looked at the pregnancy test in her hand.

Alongside his accidental career in finance, **Tim Ewins** performed stand-up comedy for eight years. He also had a very brief acting stint (he's in the film *Bronson*, somewhere in the background) before turning to writing fiction. His novels, *We Are Animals* and *Tiny Pieces of Enid*, are published by Lightning Books and he lives with his wife, son and dog near Bristol. Find Tim via the links below:

https://www.amazon.co.uk/stores/Tim-Ewins/author/B07PPLQG7Z

Twitter/X: @EwinsTim

Instagram: @tiny_pieces_of_tim

THE ARCHIVIST

PHILIPPA EAST

I arrived at St Saviour's & George's just as the caretaker was leaving. His motorbike stood roaring in the wide gravelled driveway; I could smell the hot fumes through my open car window.

'Rebecca McMasters?' he shouted over the throb of the engine. 'I was expecting you an hour ago.'

The school stood up tall against the empty blue sky, an expanse of yellow sandstone and flashing windows. I climbed from the car, from one heat to another, catching my breath at the grandeur of the place. My damp skirt was stuck to the backs of my thighs and I wiped a film of sweat from my lip.

'I know … car trouble,' I shouted back. It wouldn't be hard to believe: the car had been on its last legs for months and after the drive up to Scotland I was surprised it hadn't given up the ghost entirely.

'I've made up rooms for you in the sanatorium, east corridor. You'll find the files and papers in the main office. We stacked them all there.' He tugged his helmet down over his red hair and beard and revved the engine. 'The nearest shop's down in the village. The contractors are due to start tomorrow, so that'll give you tonight to yourself at least.'

Perhaps he was being ironic, I thought. Scottish humour is tricky.

'Won't you be back before then?' I was feeling the size and emptiness of the place.

The caretaker looked at me through his open visor, a small window. 'No chance. I'll be glad if I never set foot in this place again. Here. Keys.' He tossed the jangling set towards me and I caught the glinting bundle – just.

He gunned his engine and pushed down the visor. The heat from the bike made the air shimmer as he skidded his way towards the gates, kicking up a cloud of gravel behind him. I raised a hand to rub the grit from my eyes. The whine of his engine hung in the air long after he was out of sight; the grounds stretched away to the heavy rows of pine trees that circled the place.

Now there was only me.

The school had been closed for almost five years, but legal wrangling and some court case or other meant that, until recently, no one had been allowed to touch the place. Maybe no one had wanted to touch the place either because of what had happened here: the young pupil's tragic death. I remembered skimming headlines about it at the time – just skimming though; that wasn't part of my job. Anyway, now the contractors were finally moving in, ready to gut the classrooms and offices to make way for luxury flats. Once all trace of the school's history was removed, its past would be too. That's how these things usually worked.

I dragged my suitcase out of the car and locked the boot after me. I wondered whether I should find somewhere tidier to park the old thing, instead of right here in front of the grand entrance. On the other hand, who was here to see? Only the caretaker, kind enough to wait, but gone now too. What I hadn't told him was the real reason for my delay. It was almost too much of a cliché to say out loud: woman pulls over to the side of the road for a crying jag. Anyway, my personal life was none of his business.

I hoisted my suitcase up the steps and passed through the wide doors into the mild cool of inside. The entrance hall's marble flooring was dusty under my feet, and the glass cabinets — once housing pictures and commemorations, awards and trophies — were powdered too with a faint sheen, like a hanging veil. The school had once had a reputation to uphold, but that had pretty much disintegrated by now. Now someone needed to pick over the bones of what was left, and that someone would be me.

The sanatorium, or nurse's office, was down the east corridor, just as the caretaker had said. The room had a smell familiar to me but which I couldn't quite place: sweet, but sharp – medicinal. I leaned my suitcase against the wall. He'd made up the cot in there in a manly, slapdash way, and left a plug-in kettle and a loose handful of crumpled teabags. A small fridge, the kind students take into halls, held a single pint of skimmed milk; the use-by date today. The caretaker had left me a fan too. I plugged it in and set it whirring, half comforted, half annoyed by its buzzing whine.

In the adjoining room, through a doorless doorway, was a sort of office with a shallow desk in the alcove, along with cupboards and shelving. It was passable as a workspace; I'd certainly known worse. Yes. So far, everything would do. I would bring the files down here, one stack at a time, and sort through them. In this line of work, it's essential to have a system. There's always the temptation on these jobs to rifle through everything where you find it, spilling document after document over the floor as you become engrossed in the secrets you've uncovered. But I've seen where that sort of haphazard approach ends up, and I've learned the hard way the need for a sensible order. I've perfected the art of skim reading, taking in as much as I need to know, but never, never getting involved in the nitty-gritty. David says this skill – to never look below the surface of things – can be a curse as well as a blessing. I know what he means, but I don't think I agree.

I sat on the bed and rolled my shoulders to ease out the tension – a legacy of the eight-hour drive, I supposed. There was a bolt too, I noticed now, on the inside of the main door. Despite an uneasy restlessness, an itch to get the job started and finished, I knew I should give myself this evening to rest. Yet the late afternoon sun was magnified by the thick glass and the heat in the room was stifling, even with the fan on its highest setting. I'd forgotten how long it stayed light this far north: it would be another four hours at least before the daylight faded. I stood and tugged at the sash window, but it wouldn't budge and the roller blind was a thin thing, not much good. Outside was greenery and space, room to breathe despite the still air. I locked the sanatorium and headed out.

On the front steps, I pushed loose hairs off my forehead and wished I had a hat; dark hair absorbs the sun like nobody's business. But it was cooler out here, in the open air. I could hear the whine of a plane, but when I shaded my eyes and scanned the blue sky, I couldn't see any sign of it. It was hard even to judge in which direction to look. Sometimes the sound seemed to come from low down, behind the trees, a moment later, from directly above. For one brief second, it even felt as if the noise was coming from right beside me, burrowing into my ear.

There was no denying the place was impressive, even though this private boys' school had closed so abruptly, everything abandoned. There'd been stories in the newspapers at the time, but news stories are quickly forgotten, and I've never been one to take much interest. I'm not paid enough for that.

I set off through the grounds, round the perimeter of the school. It was strange to think that in this whole school, with dormitories and classrooms for three hundred pupils, not to mention the teachers' quarters, the dining room, the offices, and caretaker's apartments – in this whole grand and echoing place, there was no one but me. Despite the blazing heat, the thought placed a cold fingertip on the ridge of my spine.

I checked my phone, half hoping, half dreading to find a missed call or message from David. Cracks were showing again; we'd parted this morning in the peak of a row, our third in as many weeks. I felt the fissures, but I wasn't prepared to look at them. Instead, I'd done what I always did, what made David angrier than ever: got in the car and left, kidding myself the whole way that I'd good reasons to take this job, a job that was taking me six hundred miles from home and meant I'd be away another whole weekend at least, a job that was paying me barely enough to cover my petrol money. Kidding myself there was a good reason, other than the need to get away.

I rubbed the corner of my eye, where it still smarted from earlier.

At the back of the school, the grounds sloped gently down, then flattened out some distance away into sports pitches: rugby, athletics, no expense spared.

These kids, a tiny voice whispered on the breeze, *they don't know they're born.*

I frowned to myself, wondering where the words had come from.

I walked closer to the looming walls of the school building, noticing now the signs of wear and tear. The western wall, the one in fullest glare of the sun, had tiny cracks running all across it. As I stared, the wall seemed to come alive before my eyes, rippling, moving, creeping. My heart shot up in my chest, but I caught myself the way I'd been taught, and forced myself to look closer, look properly. I let out my breath in a rush of relief when I realised what it was: tiny scorpions, warmed by the sun, scuttling across the sandstone, right at home.

BACK IN THE SANATORIUM, I fished a packet of instant noodles from the bottom of my suitcase and put the kettle on. Instant noodles are a godsend on jobs like these. But now I realised I had no bowl – or fork, for that matter. I poked about the shelves of the office, dislodging boxes of plasters, packs of tissues, thermometers: all sensible nursing stock, but not what I was after. In the corner was the wooden cupboard, more like a wardrobe for clothes than for medical devices or pupils' sick charts. Perhaps this was where the school nurse had kept her stash of naughty cigarettes, confiscated from the boys. Perhaps in here too, she'd stash a bowl or plate, for guilty feasts on nights when she couldn't sleep. The kettle began to keen, air squeezing through some crack in its plastic lid and its spout filling the room with bursts of hot steam. I grasped the cupboard's wooden door handles, half expecting the thing to be locked, but the panels clicked open easily enough.

From behind the doors a face – a head – stared back at me.

. . .

THE KETTLE WAS SHRIEKING, like a child with pins
stuck in it. I felt like shrieking too, in anger at
having been given such a scare. It was just a stupid
doll, and a hideous one at that: thick brown braids
and a yellow tartan dress. A frilly tam-o'-shanter
was perched on top of its porcelain head, stuck on
with a thistle pin, and the doll's hands were clasped
in front of her. When I gave her a poke, the arms
swung side to side in a crude parody of Rock-a-bye
Baby. What on earth was this thing doing in the
nurse's cupboard? Perhaps she used it to frighten
the boys.

Don't be naughty, lads, or Wee Jeanie'll get you.

In a perverse fit of rebellion, I lifted the doll
down from the shelf and set her on the table by
the bed.

The kettle clicked off and I poured the water
over broken noodles in the best container I could
find: a coffee mug. The noodles were bland and full
of chemicals but, on my empty stomach, they
would do just fine. I drank them like soup, staring at
the doll that had scared me so much only a moment
ago. She wasn't such an ugly-looking creature, I
thought now. That yellow dress was doing nothing
for her, but she had the plump cheeks and paint-

shined eyes of any self-respecting dolly. I tipped up the mug again and frowned, almost scalding myself. Amongst the frills of her tartan dress, caught in the puffed sleeves above the little clasped hands, something was stuck. At first glance it looked like a marble, blue and whorled. But as I looked closer, I saw that there was some sort of crumpled wrapper in there too. I set the mug down and reached forward. With finger and thumb I fished out the object.

A boiled sweet.

And at the moment it dislodged into my fingers, I heard a sound, sharp and blunt.

Clack.

For a moment I thought the door catch had slipped, that the bolt had sprung loose and snapped open. But the door stood closed and the keys I'd left in the lock hadn't moved. The sound didn't repeat. Perhaps I was imagining things. But I recognised now the smell that permeated the san. Aniseed.

I placed the sweet carefully on the bedside table: blue, boiled, crinkle-wrapped.

IT WAS STILL daylight when I settled into bed that evening and I read for a while by the light seeping through the thin blind. The fan droned on, doing little to cool the air. I'd tried again to lift the ancient sash window, but it was stuck fast.

I must have drifted off eventually because, when I woke, it wasn't sunlight but moonlight that was seeping into the room. My book, a tatty second-hand paperback, had fallen onto the floor and I must have kicked away the blankets in the heat because they too had slithered off the bed. The smell of aniseed was thick in the air and, in the moonlight, the doll's face next to me on the bedside table had taken on a crooked, lopsided look, as if someone had painted on a sneer.

I switched the bedside lamp on and the little rosebud mouth and plump cheeks returned.

I lay back on the flat pillow and looked at her. She regarded me silently, giving nothing away. I left the lamp on and closed my eyes. There was no sound but the groan of the fan. I lay there feeling the breeze, seeing the moonlight through my eyelashes. The fan made a soft knocking, its mechanism clunking each time it rotated.

Half-awake, half-asleep, I can't tell if I spoke aloud or only thought the question inside my own head: 'Who's there?'

The knocking came again, a little harder this time; now it sounded like a small hand tapping at the door, soft but persistent, and with it came words

I can only have imagined: *Go away, go away, go away*.

And then a quick, bright thought, the last before I fell into the full dark of sleep: *Scorpions? But there would be no scorpions here.*

IN THE MORNING I woke early. The heat was back with a vengeance.

I made myself a milky tea from the supplies the caretaker had left and got down to work. The night had been hazy, full of strange dreams. I wondered what time the contractors and workmen would arrive, and in the same moment, I realised I hadn't called David. I sent him a hurried text: *arrived safe, heat up here is something else.* I tried to think of something more to say, something a bit more forgiving, but the stubborn part of me wasn't ready yet to apologise.

The files in the main staff office were easy enough to find. The cabinets had been broken open long before and the usual stuff lay in piles throughout the room. Insurance policies, class timetables, and minutes from staff meetings. Plus the files on each pupil, all two hundred and eighty-three of them. I took the largest stacks I could carry down to the sanatorium and set them out on the desk in the little office room. To begin with I put the fan on, but it blew the papers around too much. Instead, I stripped off down to my vest top and hitched my skirt up as high as was decent. Every half an hour or so, I'd make my way to the main school office and bring another armful back.

With the window closed and the fan off, the smell of aniseed was stronger than ever. The smell seemed to come from the doll, probably something to do with the sweet stuffed in her dress. I looked around now for the little blue candy, but couldn't spot it anywhere. Perhaps it had rolled under the bed or I'd thrown it out with last night's rubbish. I made a mental note to get down to the village today. I couldn't keep living on instant noodles. I knew myself, and how engrossed I could get in a job. The brain needs calories too. If I got in supplies for breakfasts and lunches, then I could have dinners in a nearby pub; there must be one around here somewhere.

As I worked, I felt my knots of tension ease. This is dull work, but it suits me: putting these documents in some sense of order, for someone else to decide what to keep or throw away. In all these piles and stacks of paper, only two things caught my attention. Firstly, in every pupil's file, near the back, there was a section marked off by a red divider. This section was labelled *Discipline*. In every case, this section was empty and appeared to have been hastily cleared: little scraps of paper still clung to the binders.

The second thing was the dates: dates of birth that let me calculate the boys' ages. Nineteen the oldest and the youngest, six.

He didn't stand a chance, the little voice said.

In the space at the back of my eyes I could feel the creepings of a headache. This heat, it was relentless. When I pressed my palms to my eyes, spots danced behind my eyelids. And sitting there, at the desk in the alcove, blind for a moment, that's when I heard it. Faint, warbling. If I hadn't had such sharp ears I might have mistaken it for birdsong. But when I thought about it, I hadn't seen any birds round here, not even a sparrow. So it wasn't bird song, but it was singing.

I opened my eyes. The tune was louder now. Like the smell of aniseed, it was something I recognised from long ago, from when I lived up here, when I was a kid. I could make out the words now.

Ally bally, ally-bally bee
Sittin' on yer mammie's knee
Greetin' for a wee bawbie
Tae buy some Coulter's Candy

It's a radio, I told myself, someone's left a radio on somewhere, some local station, playing Scottish folk songs. Or one of the workmen has arrived; it's someone outside, whistling, singing to themselves.

I did a stupid thing then. I shouted hello, as if there really was someone else there in that deserted school, someone I could blame for that eerie song. The pounding in my head was worse now, and that pounding was saying *the doll, the doll*.

I got up from the desk, scraping back my chair, pulling myself round the edges of the doorway. I got there just as the music stopped and the doll's arms swung back to where they belonged, hands clasped innocently in her lap. And I almost could have believed that I'd imagined the whole thing, that it was the heat and the headache confusing me, setting my imagination running wild, if in the next moment, I didn't hear that heart-pinching *clack*, and see that blue boiled sweet tumble out of the sleeves of the yellow dress, hard as a stone, as if she was trying to throw it at me.

I GRABBED my purse and the car keys, and got outside to the car. The engine was sluggish to start and, as I sat there turning and turning the ignition, the engine overheated and protesting, it felt like the whole school was leaning down over me, pressing down on the top of my head. I didn't dare look up, dreading what I might see staring from those glassy windows. At last the ignition caught and I gunned the engine and wrenched the car round the gravel drive. I didn't breathe properly until I was out of those gates, and beyond the perimeter of pine trees; in fact I didn't breathe easy until I'd driven all the way to the village and parked in an ordinary-looking car park, with ordinary-looking people going about their business all around me.

Stupid, so stupid.

I went to a cafe and ordered a sandwich. My stomach clenched at the first few bites: I hadn't felt how hungry I was. *Skipping breakfast*, I could hear David's voice saying, *come on, Rebecca, you know that's not good*. I ate and I made myself think, picking apart my confusion, my panic. You're jumping, I told myself, you're assuming. Wait, think, take it step by step.

Logic swam back to me in a cool wave. The doll, of course, was a wind-up doll that sang and swung, dispensing sweeties. The key must not have been fully unwound, and had slipped and played the song. It explained the sweetie I'd found last night, and the other one that had emerged with a clack this morning.

And the scorpions? A different voice in my head asked. Well of course they weren't scorpions, they were lizards. Scuttling in the heat, and hiding away in the cool of the morning. Lizards. An easy mistake to make.

I finished the whole sandwich and went to the store. I stocked up on bread, cheese, cereal, milk – enough to see me through the next few days. The store had air conditioning and I stood in the freezer aisle for as long as I could, letting its cool sink into my skin. When I returned to the car, my old banger, the world felt calmer. I had obligations. I had a job, I was a professional.

I put the food in the boot, and drove back.

My phone jittered as I turned up the driveway, but stopped before I could pull up. David's picture showed on the screen. I parked in front of the school and pressed the recall button, noticing how quickly my heart was beating.

David's voice, when he answered, was brisk and gruff. 'Rebecca?'

'Just missed you. I was driving back from the village.'

'We said we'd check in. I need to know how you're doing.'

The distance down the line felt vast and echoey. I climbed out of the car, the phone in one hand, keys in the other. 'Oh, you know. It's really hot.'

'Yes, you said.'

Right. My text. I retrieved the shopping from the back of the car and locked the doors behind me. 'There's just me here at the moment,' I went on, 'but I've already got started.'

'That's good.'

'Yep.'

There was a pause.

'I'm sorry about before,' he said. Sometimes David apologises on my behalf. It's a sort of arrangement we've come to.

I climbed the steps into the atrium. 'It doesn't matter,' I told him. 'Not now.'

'So when do you think you'll be up there till?'

'Monday morning at the latest, I hope.'

There was another silence on the line as I walked down the corridor towards the san. Then: 'Rebecca? How about I come join you? We could spend the rest of the weekend together, some of next week. I could book us a nice hotel. You know, make a little holiday of it.'

The headache from this morning was starting up again.

Don't let him come here.

I shook my head to clear the thought.

'Could do,' I said carefully.

'Will you think about it at least?'

I could feel the disappointment through the handset. The gap between us stretched a few miles wider. Too wide. I gripped the phone.

'David—' I blurted. 'I found this doll.'

'This what?'

'A doll. There's a doll here, in the room where I'm sleeping.'

'OK …' David's voice was cautious. 'Well, maybe it belonged to one of the boarders.'

I pictured her: frills, plaits, rosebud mouth. 'I don't think so … David, it sings a nursery rhyme. Coulter's Candy.'

'Coulter's Candy, huh?'

Make him shut up.

I shook my head again and pinched the bridge of my nose.

'Look, never mind. I don't know why I'm telling you this.'

'Rebecca, it's all right. We should talk, you can talk to me'

'It's nothing, it's stupid. Look I'll ring you later.'

And I hung up.

.   .   .

185

INSIDE THE SAN, I put the shopping bags down on the floor. I was breathing hard and could almost feel my pulse in my mouth. The doll was right there where I'd left her, still and silent. I lifted her up and felt through the layers of her dress, the ribbons and bows at the back, until finally, thankfully, my fingers closed upon what I'd hoped to find all along: the wind-up key.

I sank down on the bed, shivering with relief. That was all she was. A wind-up doll, with a mechanism that slipped.

I grasped the key and twisted it, unwinding its coils. The familiar tune started up again and the stiff arms swung back and forth.

Poor wee Jeanie was gettin' awfy thin,
A rickle o' bones covered ower wi' skin…

I kept up the pressure on the key, turning every last note out of it. I kept it turning until it wouldn't turn any more. No chance of it slipping now. I put her back where I'd found her and shut the cupboard doors tight. I texted David: *I'm all right.*

I made myself a coffee this time, strong and black.

Then I got back to work.

. . .

THE NEXT MORNING I was woken by my phone. It was the caretaker, ringing to tell me the workmen were postponing for a week. Did I need anything, he asked. Would I be all right there on my own?

I sat up in bed and shrugged. 'Why wouldn't I be?'

There was a silence on the line, like he was waiting for me to take my words back. When I didn't say anything else he grunted and hung up.

It was too hot to eat any breakfast and I knew if I didn't push on with the work this morning, the headache that was lurking behind my eyes would be here too soon for me to work much past lunchtime. Once again, I carried stacks of papers and files from the main office to the san and sifted through them one by one. Painstaking work, but it was me at my best.

St Saviour's & George's, it seemed, had been an exemplary school. Unruly behaviour was rarely a problem. The older boys helped the teachers to keep things in hand.

He let Jenks's scorpion out. Prize pet scorpion.

I didn't know where these thought fragments were coming from. It was like someone kept twiddling a radio knob in my head, picking up random bandwidths.

Scorpions again though, I noted.

At lunchtime I had another coffee. The headache somehow was keeping at bay. It was so quiet here. No workmen, no wind. I'm not sure quite where the impulse came from, in fact, I hardly even realised what I was doing until it was done, and the doll had been rescued from the cupboard and was resting once again on the bedside table, smiling softly with her little red mouth.

She was sitting there when I found the letter. The one from the local hospital doctor to the school nurse, Miss Aitkin. He hoped he was not speaking out of turn, he wrote, but he was concerned about the recent referrals. He knew lads could be lads, rowdy and clumsy at the best of times, but the injuries he had been asked to treat, perhaps they had another cause, did Miss Aitkin catch his drift?

Clipped to this letter, so neatly typed on official hospital stationery, was a sheet of writing paper, Miss Aitkin's own, it seemed, for there was no school letterhead.

Dear Doctor, said its hand-written scrawl, *I would beg you not to question—*

And there it ended.

COME HIGH AFTERNOON, it was simply too hot to work. I snapped elastic bands round the papers that were still lying loose, and switched on the fan. I stripped down to my underwear, lay flat on the bed and closed my eyes. My sleep was a thick weight. When I woke, my mouth was parched like a wrung-out sponge. I was dehydrated, I realised. I hadn't been drinking properly in all this heat.

I lay there hardly breathing, facing the wall, not turning round. I slid my hand under the pillow to where my phone was, to where I always kept it these days when I slept.

Right away, I called David. He didn't pick up the first time but, instead of leaving a message, I kept ringing. Ringing and ringing.

When at last he answered, there was such a noise in the background, a thrumming, like he was in a train or a car.

Despite the racket, I spoke in a whisper. 'David?'

'Rebecca – what is it?'

Still without turning over, I held the phone up in the hot air above my shoulder.

Ally bally, ally-bally bee
    Crawlin' roond on hand an' knee …

I pressed the phone back to my ear. 'Can't you hear it? Tell me you can hear it.'

'Hear what? Rebecca——'

'Turn that noise off. Listen!'

… Begging to yer poor mammie
Tae gi' you Coulter's Candy

The song was loud, wailing. I didn't remember this verse. I didn't know these words.

'Rebecca?' His voice was so blurred, so crackly. Where was he, what was he doing?

'Listen!' I hissed. 'Listen!'

I held the phone there, until I was sure he'd have heard, then wrenched myself over in the bed, forcing myself once again to look, to really *see*, like everyone kept telling me.

When I turned over, the doll was silent. Stock still.

I threw down the phone and grabbed her by her frilly dress and tried to find the key that wound her up but even though I searched and searched and in the end turned her right upside down so her skirts fell over her head, there was no sign of the mechanism that had reassured me so much.

The line was clearer when I picked up the phone again.

'Rebecca, what is it?' Miles away, I heard him trying to stay calm. 'What am I supposed to hear?'

I sat down on the bed and took a deep breath. 'Nothing. There's … nothing there.'

David's voice came to me across a long, long distance. 'Rebecca, please. I think you know what this is.'

My head was pounding. 'What?'

'I found your medication. You left it at home—'

Clack.

I hung up.

I DIDN'T TAKE a single break in my work for the rest of the day. I had to get it finished. My headache was stinging my eyes, but I worked on through, unearthing more secrets that I filed to one side, in a careful bundle that I marked only *The San*. There were pieces coming together, stories joining up, but I worked like an automaton, taking nothing in, for none of this was mine, and none of these failures had been my fault.

ABOUT ELEVEN I reached the end. I took everything back to the main office and lined it up neatly, filed in the archivist's system, ready to be disposed of or kept at will. Back in the san, I fell exhausted onto the bed, without even properly undressing. I hadn't had a wash, I realised, for three days now.

I did fall asleep, despite the heat; I mean I must have done because of the nightmare. I say it was a nightmare now, but part of me still wonders if it wasn't real, if everything that happened to me in that school wasn't real, though the doctor later put it all down to another episode, brought on by heatstroke and lack of food.

I dreamed, or I woke; what difference does it make? In sleep or in waking, I was sitting upright on the bed, my legs stuck out straight before me. The doll was there on the bedside table, a caricature of me, or me of it, my hands clasped and my arms moved by a force outside of me, swinging from side to side.

I was a puppet, a doll, a robot, and then the knocking came, and it was knocking, but it was a clacking too, and I saw sweet after sweet come rolling out of the doll: from her sleeves, her hair, her skirts, her mouth. They fell out and rolled off the table and the floor was covered with them, like a sea of marbles; if you tried to walk on them, you'd break your legs.

I was sitting up and I was lying down and in the dream I was sick, but in other dreams I was the nurse, and the knocking went on and I knew I should get up and open the door, I knew who was on the other side, I knew what the doctor had warned of in his letter and what a teacher had raised in a report and what, in the end, I had turned a blind eye to.

Knock, clack, knock, clack, and my arms swung back and forth with a life of their own and the doll swung and sang, and knocked and clacked, and through it all, my head pressed into the pillow, I felt the pressure building. A sweet was pushing, pushing out against my ribcage, it was pushing to burst my own lungs, and I knew if I let the boy in what I would see, the haemorrhage that didn't show on the outside, but he'd complained of stomach pains and said he couldn't breathe, and if I opened the door, there'd be no getting away from what had happened to him: no accident, of course, but the brutal beating in the dormitory, by Jenks and all his friends, for letting the scorpion out. And the pain in my head shrieked:

Open the door!
Don't open the door!
The doctor!
The nurse!
You told them not to be naughty! You told them, Wee Jeanie warned!

I couldn't breathe, but I must have screamed,

and then the sanatorium door handle turned and the sanatorium door was opening.

WHEN I CAME TO, it was broad daylight. I was lying on my side on the bed in the sanatorium, and David was there. He propped me up and held a mug of water to my mouth.

'I finished it, David. The work's all done.'

'Drink. Just keep drinking.' He slipped a pill in with the water too.

I looked around for the doll. There was no sign of her. Through in the little office, the cupboard doors were tight closed.

'I read about it,' said David. 'What happened here. The beatings, the violence.'

'The boy,' I said. 'He was only six.'

'Yes.'

'He died.'

'That's right. Outside the nurse's office. The caretaker found him.'

'She knew,' I said. 'She knew, that's the worst thing. But she didn't do anything. Her door was locked.'

David let that one go. 'I've arranged an appointment for you. When we get home.'

I closed my eyes and let the tears slide down my nose. I nodded.

He helped me up. He'd already packed my suitcase, thrown away the food, and the floor was clear, I noticed. There were no sweets.

'Did you find the doll?' I asked.

David shook his head.

Outside, the air was so still, the world looked like a photograph. David's car was parked beside mine.

'We can leave yours,' he said. 'I've spoken to a friend, he'll come pick it up.'

He opened the passenger door and helped me in. It was only when I sank into the cracked leather that I realised how weak and sick I felt. I couldn't think of the last time I'd eaten, and there was a whining ring in my ears, the kind I got when my blood pressure was low and my iron levels were through the floor. I dropped my face into my hands. No wonder, I thought, that I'd had such bad dreams. No wonder I had been hallucinating.

And the pills, I'd stopped the pills. How many times, the same thing. I felt like crying.

David loaded my suitcase into the boot, and then climbed into the driver's seat beside me. His movements, his body, were so familiar to me, I felt a choking rush of love, the kind I hadn't felt in weeks.

He had come, he'd seen what I couldn't, he'd broken my fall, like every other time before.

David started the engine and set the air con on full. I shut my eyes, waiting for the jolt as we pulled away, the haunting over, going home.

I opened my eyes. We hadn't moved. David was staring in the rear-view mirror, staring at something, I couldn't tell what. I reached out for him. 'What is it?'

The sun was a glare on the windscreen, the seatbelt was tight across my chest. David shook his head, like shaking something away. I twisted and craned my neck to see, looking over my shoulder, back at St Saviour's & George's. I passed a hand in front of my eyes, my vision unsteady and blurred. What was it, that thing? It was like a small creature, a mouse or spider, moving jerkily down the steps as if being pushed or pulled, moving like that though there wasn't a breath of wind.

As it came nearer, I made out the colour – blue – and the texture – crinkled.

A sweetie paper.

David wrenched the handbrake, released the clutch.

'Let's get out of here,' he said.

***

PHILIPPA EAST GREW up in Scotland and originally studied Psychology and Philosophy at the University of Oxford. After graduating, she moved to London to train as a Clinical Psychologist and worked in NHS mental health services for over ten years. Her debut novel *Little White Lies* was shortlisted for the CWA Dagger for best debut of 2020, and she has since published three further psychological thrillers: *Safe and Sound, I'll Never Tell* and *A Guilty Secret*. Philippa lives in the Lincolnshire countryside with her spouse and cat, and alongside her writing she continues to work as a psychologist and therapist. You can find out more about Philippa via the links below:

https://www.amazon.co.uk/stores/Philippa-East/author/B07S3JQDGK

Twitter/X: @philippa_east

Instagram: @philippa_east_author

Facebook: @philippa_east_author

NOTE: *The Archivist* was first published in *New Ghost Stories III* from The Fiction Desk.

AFTERWORD

We do hope you have enjoyed reading the stories in this collection. We have certainly enjoyed writing them. If you would like to spread the word, do tell your friends and – if you have time – consider adding a rating or review for *UnBound* on Amazon.

There have been so many people involved in creating this anthology. With huge thanks first of all to all the authors who contributed their precious stories: without them, this anthology would not exist. We are also so grateful to Samantha Brownley, brilliant champion of all things bookish, for acting as our proofreader and catching all those pesky typos that somehow always manage to slip through.

Huge thanks again to Gina Wynn (www. ginawriteswords.com) who formatted both our first anthology *UnLocked* and this second anthology. The gorgeous layout and typesetting you'll find within these pages is all credit to her. We are also eternally grateful to fellow author Heleen Kist who created our stunning cover, based on an original design by Emma Bailey. Heleen, your incredible generosity in supporting this project is hugely appreciated.

Lastly, thank you so much to you: our readers. It is in your hands that our stories truly take flight. By purchasing this anthology, you are also supporting the brilliant work of adult literacy charity Read Easy (CC 1151288). You can find out lots more about Read Easy, the adults they have helped learn to read, and their work via https://readeasy.org.uk.

I hope that the D20 Authors will continue to write and publish long into the future. If you would like to keep up to date with all our boundless (☺) achievements, we'd be delighted to connect with you on Twitter/X: @TheD20Authors, and don't forget to check out all our latest D20 books via our affiliate link to the Bookshop page: https://uk.bookshop.org/shop/TheD20Authors.

Happy reading! Here's to being UnBound.

Philippa East and the D20 Authors